DISCLAIMER

This is a work of fiction. Almost all names, characters, business, events and incidents are the products of the author's imagination. Any resemblance to actual persons, living or dead, or actual events is purely coincidental - with the exception of the mention of Dr. Stephen Hawking (to explain the concept of time), and Willard Scott (to lend his meteorological assistance), who are respectfully mentioned in this narrative to advance the storyline.

PREFACE

Dear Reader,

My name is Thomas Dean Brennan, former mayor of Dublin, Tennessee. I say former mayor because I'm dead. I'm a ghost, a phantom, a spirit. I have no corporeal body, only my consciousness which seems to function according to a law of physics undiscovered and unexplained by humanity to date, despite thousands of years of observance, study and scientific research. When I inhabited the world in which you currently live, I did some bad things, but I managed to redeem myself and eventually was allowed to move on. I now have peace and freedom and can travel wherever I wish, but I'm constantly drawn back to little Dublin where I lived most of my life. It's a lovely town, but just like everywhere on your side of Paradise, it has its problems (remember, I was one of them). My wife Janet, who predeceased me, is curious about my obsession for wanting to help Dubliners out; after all, aren't they supposed to work out their issues like we did? But I believe I'm guiding, not fixing.

Anyway, let me tell you a little about Dublin. Located south of Knoxville and Oak Ridge in northeastern Tennessee, our fair city was first settled by and for the Irish railroad workers and their families in the late nineteenth century. The railroads ran from the eastern seaboard, through Dublin and other small towns, to Memphis and beyond. In its heyday, rail was king for shipping and travel. Commerce here grew to accommodate not only the original residents, but also the many people drawn to the area because of its beauty - gentle and fertile rolling hills and valleys, lakes and streams, and magnificent forests. Although several state highways run in every direction near Dublin, trucks and cars whiz by, their drivers are usually unaware of its existence. That's changing, though, as you'll see.

One last thing: Time in the Hereafter is non-existent. What you understand as days and years is actually inaccurate. People have followed the seasons and the track of the sun and stars to give their lives order ever since there were humans living in clans, tribes, and larger communities. But time is not linear; everything is actually happening all at once. Stephen Hawking explained quantum physics to us during a recent lecture, so I'm not talking off the top of my head (so to speak). Therefore, the chapters that follow aren't presented in a strict calendar-based manner; they overlap like leaves fallen from a tree. If you don't understand, it's not important. I just wanted to brag about meeting Stephen Hawking. Thanks for stopping, and enjoy your stay.

-1-

Father McCarthy's Vision

Father Shane McCarthy was devoted to his calling at Saint Isidore the Farmer Catholic Church. His duties were many and varied, but a funeral was always delicate to officiate. Not that he personally was ever sad for the deceased as that soul was at peace; but it was sorrowful for the family and friends, as was the case this morning. Donaghan Ryan lay in his beautiful mahogany casket awaiting burial in Dublin's Catholic cemetery.

Don's son, Beauregard Ryan, with his wife, Grace, and children filled the front pew. Beau's eyes wandered from the casket's white brocade pall, to the ornate crucifix behind the altar, then back again to the casket. He and his parents had always been close, but now they both were gone. He wondered if they would be proud of him now, having been elected mayor after Dean Brennan's death. A tear rolled down the side of his nose - of course they would be.

The pews were filled with Don Ryan's friends and numerous relatives; everyone wanted to say goodbye and show their thanks for his kind assistance through the years.

Father McCarthy caught the mayor's eye and gave him a brief nod, which was returned.

"Dear family and friends, we gather here together to not only celebrate the life of Donaghan Ryan, but to help him attain his final reward with our prayers," the priest began. "For those of you who have not attended a Catholic funeral mass before, please don't feel embarrassed by not knowing the ritual of standing and kneeling; you're not obligated to participate. Stay seated and don't worry about it."

There were a few chuckles, then Father McCarthy assumed his role and nodded to the altar boys to begin the service. It was ritualistic and peaceful. The priest's reflections of the Honorable Donaghan Ryan reminded the attendees of his unwavering support of Saint Isidore's for many years, and the pro bono services the Ryan Law Firm had provided his clientele, if necessary. The priest anointed the casket with incense to assist the congregants' prayers rising to Heaven on the smoke, and at the end of the service, he provided communion for those who desired it.

But while Father McCarthy offered communion, he happened to look up and lost his concentration when an apparition appeared next to the draped casket on its trolley. The apparition was not unknown to the priest; indeed, most of the congregation had met or dealt with former Mayor Dean Brennan sometime during his thirty-five years as the elected head of Dublin. He wondered if he was hallucinating, or was Brennan really there, touching the casket and apparently speaking with its occupant.

Mustering his rational thoughts and tearing his eyes away from the image, the priest conducted the remainder of the funeral with calm and grace, and when it was time for the casket to be moved, the apparition had disappeared. Breathing a sigh of relief, he took his place in the procession down the aisle and prayed with all his heart that the former mayor had not returned for good. It was an egregious wish, especially while in the middle of a funeral, but although he was a priest and a messenger of God's word, he was also a man and, therefore, imperfect.

Things went to plan at the cemetery and the weather was lovely, shining and warm. Father McCarthy performed the Rite of Committal, sprinkling holy water as Don Ryan's body was committed to the grave. But as he said, "earth to earth, ashes to ashes, and dust to dust", he looked at the crowd and saw Dean Brennan standing behind everyone. Dean smiled when he caught the priest's eye. Luckily, two men caught the priest as he fainted. It would have been embarrassing for him to fall into the grave.

Of course I had to attend Don's funeral. To not go would have been a disgrace. My wife Janet tried to talk me out of it, but for once I didn't listen. Don and I had been good friends almost all our lives and I wanted to be the one who led him into The Great Beyond. And it's a good thing I showed up because I didn't notice any other spirits. He might have had to hang around like I did without a guide, although I couldn't imagine any strings tying him down, as they had me. Anyway, I told Don how to propel his spirit by thinking about where he wanted to go, and explained some of the unknown laws of physics he'd need. It was great to see him again. I guess I did unnerve Father McCarthy, though. Strange he was the only one who saw me; I guess he's more sensitive than most people. I'll have to remember that in the future.

-2-

Morningsong Family Meeting

"All right, everybody, did you grab some breakfast? If not, there's food at the bar and coffee and tea over on that table," called out Barney Morningsong, owner of The Golden Goblet Tavern, and elected head of the large Morningsong family. He chatted with a few people while waiting for everyone to get their food and settle down at the tables. This early in the morning the tavern wasn't open; there were just a few employees in the kitchen preparing for the lunch crowd when the tavern opened at eleven.

"Well, as you know, we're meeting to discuss what Mother and I have been working on for a while, that being the 1878 land grab of Cherokee land. Mother, you wanted to talk to the family first, so let me attach this microphone to your collar so you don't have to speak loudly."

Old Mrs. Morningsong was a fixture in Dublin. The little woman who always dressed in long, colorful skirts, was at least ninety years old. She didn't worry about something as trivial as age; it wasn't important. When her eleven children were born, her age on their birth certificates varied. Townsfolk called her Mrs. Morningsong, but her given name was Awinita, or "fawn" in Cherokee. It was a good name. As a child, she had large brown eyes and long lashes, and could slip through the forest without making a sound. She had outlived two husbands, so she made sure to marry a younger man the third time. He, Enoli, sat quietly now, watching and listening, solemn and still.

"My dear family," she began, as Barney stepped back, "although I'm happy we're together, unfortunately, this is not a celebration. Today we're here to consider a matter of great importance. As many of you know, my grandfather, Truth-Teller Morningsong, was born in 1828, a member of the Eastern Cherokee tribe. When he was only ten years old,

his family hid away in North Carolina with hundreds of Cherokee to avoid being forced to relocate a thousand miles to the Indian Territory west of the Mississippi River. They were lucky; there was much hardship and death on the Trail of Tears. Truth-Teller became a young man, then a father, then chief of his tribe, until he was elected Chief of the Seven Cherokee Nations in 1870. He was only forty-two, but very wise and respected because he lived up to his name." Here she paused and turned to her son. "Barney, you can take over now."

Barney clipped the microphone to his polo shirt collar and read from a sheaf of papers. "Because the Intercontinental Railway had been completed in 1869, more and more rail spurs were built. These railways cut through federal Indian lands and numerous fights broke out. Dubliners know our arc of railway was built by immigrant Irish, but they forget who occupied the land to begin with. The Indian never felt he owned the land; it was loaned to him by The Creator to care for and protect. Yet, the railways were built without asking permission from the land's occupants.

"When the Morning Glory Bed and Breakfast was renovated, a strongbox was found which contained the original deed to the house and grounds - thousands of acres. A Pennsylvania lumberman, realizing the vast forestlands of East Tennessee would make him much richer, decided to build a home here. One railroad spur he had a stake in ran through this area and, since it could move the lumber, he illegally wheedled the land from the local Cherokee with a handshake, some cheap trades, and a promise to allow them to continue to live here. He didn't purchase it because the Indians didn't consider the land theirs to own or sell. But, of course, this Fredrick B. Worthington didn't tell the truth. Worthington built homes and farmsteads for himself and several members of his family. Outraged, the Cherokee in the area burned down all of the houses except one, sending the occupants packing, then sent a message to Chief Truth-Teller Morningsong in North Carolina. In turn, Truth-Teller wrote a letter to the Commissioner of Indian Affairs, William Nicholson, in Washington, DC.

"The following year, in 1879, Worthington, who had stubbornly refused to leave the remaining house, received a letter from Commissioner Nicholson, requesting an explanation of why he hadn't gone through the proper channels for acquiring land. Not that it would have changed the outcome, but at least the Indians wouldn't have had a legal chance to retaliate. But Truth-Teller pronounced he would fight, and sued Worthington for having stolen the land from the Cherokee people. Finally unnerved, Worthington wisely decided not to tempt fate, and eventually abandoned his house and his lumber business in that area.

"It took several years, but the Cherokee were finally able to reclaim their land. [1] Truth-Teller's children kept the story alive as a song, but it was never written down and, therefore, was unknown by generations of farmers who continued to purchase tracts of land from developers who assumed it was theirs to sell.

"Mother, a few of you, and I have been trying to wrap our heads around this situation for a couple of years now. To be truthful, I don't know if there will ever be a good solution, but several of us will be meeting with the Principal Chief of the Eastern Band of Cherokee Indians in three weeks. If any of you are interested in going to North Carolina with us, let Tallulah know so we can make motel reservations. We plan to spend one night." Barney's daughter raised and waved her hand as if to say, "Here I am."

Barney looked at his wristwatch and said, "If anyone has comments or questions, I'll be around here all day. But it's almost time to open the bar, so all you underaged folks need to leave," he said, winking at his step-father, Enoli. "We'll share travel details later."

-3-

The House on Morning Glory Lane

In the 1840s, Horace Greeley, founder of the New York Tribune newspaper, urged determined, energetic souls to "Go West, young man, and grow up with the country." The phrase reverberated through the rest of the 19th century, repeated many times until it became a mantra. By the end of the century, a twenty-year-old Brooklyn grocery clerk named Nate Vogel took his advice as had thousands of ambitious young men before him. Many went to prospect for riches, many bought farmland, some were just curious and adventurous. Nate didn't get as far west as he thought he would have to, as once the train crossed the Appalachian mountains and traveled south, he fell in love with the State of Tennessee and disembarked in the new town of Dublin.

Nate opened N. Vogel Groceries in 1900, living above the store. For the time, it was ambitious; one rather large room stocked with canned foods and staples such as flour, sugar and dried beans, plus candies and spices many townsfolk had never seen before. He bought or bartered for fresh products such as eggs, milk, and fresh produce from the local farmers. Nate stuck to what he knew and did well for himself.

When Clara Jacobs, also from New York, began shopping at N. Vogel Groceries, she and Nate fell in love. Clara's father had also decided to take his chances in the West, and brought his family to a nearby town to open a tailor's shop. The Jacobses approved and became fond of Nate, and he and Clara married. Nate purchased Worthington's large abandoned house which they set out to upgrade, and within five years, they were very busy between the grocery store and raising three sons, Abraham, Benjamin and Caleb.

When the boys were old enough, they learned a trade. Abe became a county surveyor and moved to the Clinch Valley area which was populated with farms and small communities, but ready to grow. He married and settled down there.

Benjamin enjoyed the grocery business and worked with his father at N. Vogel Groceries, taking over the business when his parents moved back east. He married and raised several children. Howard, his firstborn son, inherited the business when Ben retired, refreshed the store inside and out, and renamed it Fresh Street Market. He added a wider variety of brands and hired several general helpers, one of whom was young Quentin Flatbush who quickly learned the ins and outs of retail selling. When Howard retired early due to health problems, none of his children chose to run the market, so he helped Quentin purchase the business from him.

Caleb had become a pharmacist, opened a pharmacy, and served the town until his wife became ill. Although he wasn't close to retirement age, Cal decided to sell the pharmacy to be with and care for his wife. Because Quentin was doing so well with The Fresh Market, he bought the pharmacy, employing two pharmacists from other communities to manage it for him. The young man enjoyed owning two thriving businesses and, despite his young age, ran them successfully.

The years passed quickly, and Nate and Clara, now in their sixties, made the painful decision to return to New York to care for their elderly parents, with the hope that one day they would return to Dublin and live out their days with their growing family. Abe, Ben, and Cal, having established their own families and homes, weren't interested in maintaining a house as large as the one they were raised in, so Nate and Clara sold the house on Morning Glory Lane to insurance salesman John Carney, who promised to take good care of it and its lovely morning glory garden, assuring them they were welcome to visit any time.

John Carney rented a little office on Broad Street from which he ran Carney Insurance. He sold every type of insurance and did well - so well that he eventually hired an office assistant to take calls and make appointments. Her name was Olivia Doyle. She was bright, and very pretty with her dark curls and laughing eyes; their clients loved her. John loved her, too, and they married hoping to fill the big house with a large and happy family. But although the house stood at the ready, they were never blessed with children. Although it was a tremendous disappointment to them both, as the years went by they filled the void with volunteer and charity work. They were everyone's aunt, uncle, parent and grandparent, and with that they had to be content.

After many years together, John passed away after what he thought was just his gallbladder acting up again; he'd had a heart attack. Olivia was devastated, and only lived a few more years after the death of her beloved husband.

For her entire life, nobody, including John, ever knew the secret Olivia kept to herself - a secret revealed only after she died, but which changed the life of one man forever.

Hayden O'Mooney was Olivia's child with Thomas Dean Brennan, who would one day become mayor of Dublin. Raised by Olivia's sister and brother-in-law in another state, Hayden only learned about his birth father after inheriting Olivia's house and moving to Dublin. He never had the opportunity to meet Dean Brennan, as the mayor had passed away shortly before he arrived, but he did acquire a family he didn't know he had: three half-siblings and their children. Hayden's inheritance of the family home and a substantial sum of money turned his life around. On advice from his real estate agent, he converted the house into a bed and breakfast establishment with an artist's studio where he continued to produce his popular watercolors. Hayden married Mayor Brennan's former executive assistant, Fiona, and they were happy together, living in The Morning Glory B&B with Fiona acting as general manager. Things were running smoothly until Hayden's former wife, Lauren, came to visit.

-4-

There's a New Church in Town

As the Reverend Jacob Ezel strolled through the vacant Cleansing Waters Baptist Church building with realtor Jason Ford, his bright, dark eyes darted around assessing the space. Cleansing Waters had closed when the pastor left for greener pastures, a younger congregation and, hopefully, better wages. It was a pretty building, well-maintained inside and out. Jason kept his eye on the man, reading his body language.

"Try the acoustics," the realtor urged. "You really don't even need a microphone if you speak up."

Reverend Ezel nodded, then cleared his throat and called out, "Beloved, never avenge yourselves, but leave it to the wrath of God, for it is written, 'Vengeance is mine, I will repay', says the Lord."

The words reverberated throughout the room to his obvious satisfaction. "Thank you for the tour, Mr. Ford. I am very interested in leasing this building, and I'm going to recommend it to the Building Committee and Church Board. I'm sure they'll be as impressed as I am." He didn't mention that he was the reverend, building committee and church board all in one, since his wife had divorced him, and all their relations dropped out of the services he'd been holding in their basement.

"Excellent," Jason replied. "Please let me know what transpires and we'll finalize the paperwork if everyone is in agreement." He led Ezel out the front door and locked it. "I hope it turns out well," he said, and held out his hand.

Reverend Ezel shook Jason's hand and smiled, thinking, *I'm pretty sure everyone will be in agreement. It's time to start over.*

Two days later, Ezel called with the happy news that there were no objections about moving the church to Dublin. He made an appointment to see Jason in two days' time with the first and last month's rent, and a plan to build a new congregation for The True Faith Missionary Church.

-5-

Lauren's Visit

As Lauren O'Mooney packed her bags, ticking items off her list with a pink highlighter, her friend, Cricket, lolled on the bed, chattering and disturbing Lauren's thoughts. As if Lauren could focus.

"So there we were." Cricket was continuing a story that seemed to have no end, or beginning for that matter. "Randy and I were sitting on the beach at night in beautiful Punta Cancun, counting the waves as they swooshed in: uno, dos, tres, and so on. But I couldn't remember my Spanish any farther than twenty, so I counted to viente about five or six times while trying to remember how many times I did that until my brain felt like it was going to explode! Randy was counting the stars and I kept throwing him off, and all of a sudden, we were laughing our fool heads off! He's a great guy - too bad he's engaged to dull, old Julia. She'll anchor his dinghy." She took a deep breath. "I keep telling you, Lauren, you really should smoke a joint or two to relax. You've been so tense lately. I have a few in my purse - want one?"

Lauren shook her head no. "I don't do drugs, Cricket, you know that. I like to keep my wits about me."

Cricket tossed back her head laughing. "Lauren, I've seen you get drunk as a skunk! What wits do you keep when you're drinking?"

"Please, shut up!" Lauren snarled, list in hand, wheeling towards her friend. "Do you mind going home, please? I'm trying to pack and you're not helping me."

19

Cricket cringed at this unexpected verbal assault. With a sniff, she answered, "I was only trying to make conversation, you know. You don't have to bite my head off." Standing up, she continued with a pout, "I hope you have a great trip, Lauren. Tell old what's-his-name to keep working really hard so you and your precious art gallery can stay in business. It's the only thing you care about, isn't it?" Scooping up her bag, Cricket stomped out of the room as tears loomed in her eyes.

Lauren heard the front door slam and took a long, calming breath. Cricket was her best friend and she was ashamed of herself. Nobody's perfect, thought Lauren. Maybe Cricket is right; I'm flying to that little town again just to beg Hayden to create more artwork for me to sell. She had rarely spoken to her ex-husband in almost a year, despite his promise to keep the art coming in. Her financial future depended on what was selling, and Hayden O'Mooney's watercolors were in demand right now. How long the trend would last she didn't know, but having dealt with other artists for a number of years, she knew she had to strike while the iron was hot.

No, she wasn't looking forward to the visit. Not only was it going to be painful to discuss her financial situation with her ex-husband, but he had married the woman he'd hired as general manager of his new bed and breakfast. Lauren felt Fiona didn't like her much, but at least she'd been civil about it. She hoped they could at least remain that way for a few days while she and Hayden hashed out a formal business arrangement.

Checking her list twice, she called it quits. She only had a few last-minute items to toss into her bags tomorrow morning. Then, realizing Cricket's offer to drive her to the airport was now out of the question, she scheduled a cab to pick her up at seven-thirty in the morning. Before going to bed, Lauren did something she hadn't done in years. She knelt at the edge of her bed and sent up a prayer that this trip would be fruitful for all, and maybe even enjoyable.

It was a busy Saturday at the B&B. Hayden was on his way to the reception desk to check on arrivals when he saw Lauren's luxury rental car pull up in the circular driveway. Rosemary Zimmer greeted him with her perpetual sunny smile.

"I just called Izzy," she said. "He'll be here in a second to park the car and help the lady with her luggage."

"Thanks," Hayden smiled. "I guess I don't have to remind anybody that this guest is my ex-wife."

"No, it's about all everyone has been talking about the past few days," she admitted.

Hayden sighed as he watched Lauren attempt to tip Izzy, the bellman/go-fer, who was refusing to take her money.

"No tips," he told her, shaking his head.

"Because I'm the owner's ex-wife, I suppose," Lauren speculated.

"No, ma'am, because we don't accept tips. We're well-paid and treat everyone the same," was the reply.

"Oh, well, then ...," she said, then swooped through the double doors. Izzy followed with a rolling cart ladened with three large suitcases, a hanging bag, and several carrying cases. Hayden approached, gave Lauren a brief hug and accompanied her to the reception desk, while Izzy brought her things to the Rose Suite.

The room was inviting, bright and charming. From the double bed with its lovely sheets and quilt to the floral painting on the wall (an O'Mooney, Lauren noted), to the rug covering honey-colored wood floors, and the overstuffed chair and footstool near the window, everything was perfectly suited for an extended stay. Lauren remembered that Hayden's wife, Fiona, had furnished and decorated the room, then blushed as she also recalled how dismissively she had treated the woman on her last visit.

"The room is even lovelier than before," she said with admiration, turning to Hayden who had helped Izzy unload the luggage.

"I'll tell Fiona. She's blossoming as a decorator," said Hayden. "She isn't here at the moment, but she'll be back within the hour. In the meantime, would you like a tour of the place now that it's finished?" Lauren had previously visited when the B&B was still being renovated.

"Absolutely,!" was the reply. Lauren was pleased she had Hayden's attention for a while, although it was too soon to talk shop. She followed him around his art studio at the top of the turret, then into two unoccupied guest suites, down the wide, curved stairs to the first level, to the library, past the kitchen, sitting room, and the large and lovely solarium with its "catio" outside. The two tenants of the catio ran into the solarium to greet them; they loved being petted and admired.

"Oh, cats!" she exclaimed, hiking up her long dress so as not to be dusted with hair. Hayden took note.

"Do you not like cats, or is it just cat hair?" he asked. Funny, this was something they had never discussed before.

"I like cats, Hayden, but not their hair. This dress was quite expensive. Do you mind if we don't touch them?"

"Not at all," he answered. "We don't force them on anybody."

"Are there other animals in the building?" she asked tentatively.

"One of our guests has a therapy dog, a French bulldog," Hayden replied. "She's a good little dog."

Lauren nodded and yawned. "I should unpack my clothes before they wrinkle. Oh, no, I forgot my travel iron."

"No problem," Hayden answered. "If you need an iron, there's one in the closet."

"Well, then ...," Lauren murmured, "It's good to see you again, and this time I'm going to try to be a nicer, um, guest."

As he left Lauren in the Rose Suite to unpack and rest, he chuckled. A kinder and gentler Lauren would be refreshing, but he doubted she could pull it off for the length of her stay which, judging from the amount of baggage she has brought, could be longer than they had anticipated. He'd have to check with Rosemary.

In the kitchen, chef Curly Pete was tending to the evening meal. "Hi, Boss," he said when Hayden walked in. "Everything okay with your ex?"

"I guess the whole staff knows, don't they? That's okay, we're on speaking terms. She'll just be here a little while ...," he paused as Fiona opened the kitchen door carrying a few bags, but he pretended not to see her. "But you know, Pete, how much I love my wife."

Fiona looked at the men and set the bags down. "Talking about me while my back was turned, I see."

"Yes, ma'am," replied Curly Pete. "You shoulda heard what Mr. Hayden said about you."

Hayden just stood there grinning.

"Well then, maybe I should take some of this back to the store. I don't generally buy champagne unless it's for a special occasion."

"Don't you dare," Hayden said, taking a step forward to protect the bottles. "But what's the special occasion?"

"Our six-month wedding anniversary," Fiona answered, arching an eyebrow. "Curly Pete didn't forget, which is why I bought shrimp for an appetizer and lamb chops for the grill."

"Thank you, ma'am," said the chef, "I appreciate it. Supper will be at six". Then he put the chops and wine in the refrigerator, and headed outside to fill the grill with charcoal.

Hayden kissed Fiona lightly. "I'm sorry I forgot our anniversary. I've been thinking about Lauren's visit."

"You're forgiven," she said. "Actually, I was thinking about it, too. But I promise I'll be on my best behavior while she's here."

"That's what she said, too," he said.

"Um, where is she? I saw the rental car in the back."

"Unpacking, maybe taking a nap," he answered. "Traveling wore her out."

"Did you give her the tour?" Fiona asked.

"Inside and out," he answered, nodding. "I think she was impressed, maybe a little concerned that it occupies a lot of my day. But she did perk up when she saw my studio and the works in progress. She didn't say anything out loud, though. We're sure to have a conversation soon."

Fiona nodded. Hayden's patience and kindness would surely ease Lauren's fears about her supply of O'Mooney paintings.

"Let's go see how Curly Pete needs help with the charcoal," Hayden said, taking his wife's arm. "Since you mentioned lamb chops, I can hardly think of anything else."

Fiona winked and whispered cheekily, "Think harder."

After Lauren woke from her nap, she sat up at the edge of the bed and stretched. The window was open and she noted the distinct odor of charcoal burning. Peering out, she saw a few people wandering through arches and trellises, stopping occasionally to smell various flowers. It was a lovely scene; Claude Monet would have loved it. She wasn't a naturalist and couldn't tell a petunia from a weed, but Hayden had mentioned the cycle of the beautiful morning glory vines during her tour and she couldn't get it out of her mind. He said the flowers bloomed for just a day. Strangely, her last conversation with Cricket floated into memory. Was she stuck in a rut, not enjoying every day? Would her life be as fleeting as a morning glory flower - here today, gone tomorrow, not making a difference?

A knock on the door pulled her mind away from her reverie. "Lauren, are you awake? Dinner will be ready at six o'clock."

"I just woke up, Hayden, but I'll be down soon," she answered through the door. Her watch read five-fifteen, enough time to freshen up and change her clothes. She looked at the several large bags, realizing she still had to unpack. And she couldn't remember in which bag she'd put her casual clothes. But thirty minutes later, Lauren emerged from her room wearing a light pink jumpsuit with a flowered shrug jacket, and pink sandals. She even wore a pair of jaunty pink flamingo earrings.

Fiona met her in the dining room. "Hello, Lauren. I hope you had a good trip."

"Yes, thank you," she replied. "It's nice to see you again, Fiona."

After a moment of embarrassed silence, Fiona continued. "Since this is a bed and breakfast, our guests are generally tourists, and on their own for lunch and dinner, but," she quickly added, "of course you are a special guest, so you'll be eating with us, if that suits you."

"Yes, please," Lauren answered with relief. "I wouldn't know where to go."

"Have a seat, then, and I'll go round up Hayden. He's nearby, and supper's ready."

Lauren took a seat at the long table, admiring the table settings before Hayden brought out three goblets of jumbo shrimp cocktail and put one at each table setting. Fiona brought glasses and a bottle of cold water in a decanter.

"The cocktail sauce is chef Curly Pete's secret recipe. I keep telling him he needs to bottle and sell it, but he's reluctant to turn the recipe over to anyone," Hayden said. "In the meantime, let's enjoy it."

Finding herself licking her fingers after the appetizer was gone, Lauren blushed. "That was delicious! My compliments to the chef."

"Duly noted, ma'am," Curly Pete said as he entered the room with hot dishes of grilled lamb chops, spinach with feta, and lemon garlic potatoes. Lauren's eyebrows rose in appreciation after the man had left.

"Do you eat this well every night, Hayden? If so, The Morning Glory must be doing exceptionally well."

Fiona had left the room and returned with an uncorked bottle of champagne on ice and three fluted wine glasses. Hayden filled the glasses, then said, "We are doing very well, but we don't eat like this every night; we usually cook for ourselves. But tonight Fiona and I are celebrating our six-month wedding anniversary, so it's a special dinner to which you were cordially invited."

They all clinked their glasses together, and Lauren said, "Happy anniversary," but she didn't drink her champagne, resorting to her water glass instead.

"Lauren?" Hayden asked.

"I've given up drinking," she answered quietly. "It's been about ten months now. I'm a pariah at social events," she said with a half-hearted chuckle. "My friends laugh when I bring my own sparkling water to a party. Oh, sorry, I forgot to let you know in advance. I'll pick some up tomorrow at the grocery store."

"There's no need," Fiona said. "We always have some on hand; not everyone drinks alcohol. Sometimes you just want a little fizz. Here, give me your champagne glass and I'll swap it for fizzy water."

I really want to dislike Fiona, Lauren thought, *but she really is pleasant, and they're clearly in love.* "Thanks, Fiona, that's very kind. Now, let's eat this heavenly-smelling dinner!"

-6-

Lauren Goes to Church

Lauren woke early the following morning which was Sunday. As Hayden had told her he spends Sundays painting in his studio, she wondered what to do with her day. She thought perhaps a little ride around town would kill some time until lunch; maybe she'd find that camping place she'd read about online. After lunch she planned to run a business deal past Hayden. She showered, applied her make-up, fixed her hair, and put on a new, knee-length sheath dress with a bold print and three-quarter length sleeves. As she walked down the staircase to breakfast, she was aware that all eyes were on her. Hayden, who was chatting with one of the guests, followed everyone's gaze. He was reminded that before they married, Lauren had been a model and could still command a room without saying a word.

"Good morning, Lauren," he smiled. "You look lovely this morning. Please have a seat next to Mrs. Dixon here and Izzy will bring your tea - Earl Grey with cream, right?"

Lauren nodded. "Thank you, Hayden. It's a lovely morning, isn't it?"

Mr. Dixon, sitting on the other side of his wife, said, "It's even lovelier now, isn't it, Betty Sue?"

His wife answered by poking him in the ribs with her elbow and gave him a "look".

He laughed it off and pushed his ball cap up, revealing friendly, dark eyes. Lauren smiled and looked down at the menu. She had no intention of leading anyone on; that was something Cricket would do. Izzy brought hot water and tea bags, and took her order.

"Thank you, Izzy," she said to him, and watched him blush.

"You're welcome, Ms. Lauren," he answered, having asked how to address her. After all, calling her Mrs. O'Mooney would be confusing now that Fiona was also Mrs. O'Mooney.

The conversation around the table confirmed that most of the guests were planning a day at the campground, deciding whether they wanted to go out on the boats, visit the farm, hike a trail, and so on. Most had purchased a two-day weekend pass in order to take it all in, as well as doing some shopping in Dublin before they left.

Mr. Dixon leaned over his plate of bacon and eggs and asked Lauren what her plans were. Betty Sue Dixon glared at him.

"Daniel, it's none of your business what the lady is going to do with her day. Clearly, she's not dressed to go camping or tromp down a hiking trail."

"Pardon me, ma'am," Daniel Dixon chuckled. "It appears I'm out of bounds asking."

"Actually, it's all right," Lauren answered. "I think I'll go for a ride around town for a while, then go to church." Why did she say that? It just popped out of her mouth. She hadn't been to church in years.

"Which church?" Hayden asked with surprise.

"I ... I don't remember the name of it. I passed it on the way here; it's apparently a new place." Well, now she was locked into this.

Hayden reflected on what Lauren had just said. In all the years he'd known her, they rarely went to church. More often, they made their appearances at weddings, funerals and christenings, skipping regular services. But maybe this was something she'd been doing over the past year since their divorce, so he wisely said nothing more. If she mentioned it later, they could discuss it then.

Breakfast over, the guests went up to their rooms to prepare for the day. Lauren returned downstairs with her purse, a brimmed hat that matched her new dress, and round designer sunglasses. Car keys in hand, she sought out Fiona and Hayden, bade them goodbye, and got into her rental car. Now, which way was that church she'd seen?

Church is Open For Business

Jacob Ezel had driven into Dublin with his worldly belongings in the back seat of his compact car, and rented a long-term stay at a motel close to the commercial corner of town. If all went well, he'd be moving out of there within two months, his sights already set on Knoxville or Oak Ridge - more fish in a bigger pond. After paying the rent on the former Baptist church, he began preparing for the grand opening of the True Faith Missionary Church. Wasting no time, it took only a week to post a large sign on the church's lawn to alert neighbors and passersby that it was now "Welcoming the Faithful" with Sunday services at ten o'clock and Wednesday evening bible study. His counterfeit diploma from a prestigious bible college, mounted prominently in a large gold frame just inside the front doors, caught the eye immediately. But it may as well have said "Open For Business", for business it was to be for the false reverend.

He hadn't had time to put an ad in the local paper, a weekly printed on Monday. Just the fact he was up and running again, though, gave him purpose and a goal for next week. When several vehicles parked in the church lot around nine forty-five, Ezel was pleasantly surprised. He met the first couple at the door with an easy smile and a firm handshake, and when another couple, then a young family showed up, he met them the same way with thanks and a few words to the children.

But Ezel's heart skipped a beat when he spotted a beautiful woman entering the church. Was that a halo around her head, or just the sun shining on her auburn hair? Was she walking towards him, or was she floating? When she said, "Good morning, Reverend," he found his mouth was dry as a desert. Incapable of speech, he swallowed hard and finally managed, "Good morning, ma'am. Please come in and have a seat - there are plenty of spaces, still plenty of them, it's much cooler inside." He knew he was babbling, but he couldn't stop until, fortunately, his watch alarm chimed.

"Oh!" he exclaimed, yanking himself back to reality. "It's time for me to prepare for the service. Pardon me, please." With that, he abandoned Lauren O'Mooney at the door and hurried to his office. Opening a bottle of water and taking a gulp, his tongue unglued itself from the roof of his mouth. He suddenly wished he had something stronger than water available. What had happened, he asked himself? He couldn't afford to be off his game now that he'd invested his last dime into this scheme. Grabbing the handouts he would distribute to the attendees, Ezel took a deep breath before approaching the stage - it was time for his performance.

Without saying a word, Jake walked to the piano and sat down, surprising his audience. He closed his eyes for a moment and began to play and sing, eliciting gasps and sighs in the pews. After singing two uplifting songs about serving humanity and the Almighty that the attendees had never heard before, he moved to the lectern.

"I wrote those two songs myself, friends, because I felt we all needed to remember that the Lord will smile on us for proving our love for Him."

It was time to fire up the new parishioners. Gripping the lectern for emphasis, he said, "Friends, there is a missionary church in Somalia, on the Horn of Africa, founded by an old seminary friend of mine, Peter Vandeker. I contacted Peter recently to see how he was doing and if there was anything that I - we - can do to help his congregation. There is massive unemployment there, especially among young people; communicable diseases are spreading rapidly due to lack of health services; there has been unprecedented flooding in the past few years; and to top it off, an infestation of locusts not seen since biblical times. This is all true, from the horse's mouth. You can look online if you don't believe me."

Their hearts broke when they heard that families were trying to live on less than two dollars a day, making it impossible for their children to get the education they needed to raise their standard of living in years to come. Add that to the poor living conditions and meager healthcare facilities, and it would be apparent the situation in these African nations were dire. Ezel executed his plan: Day #1, Step #1.

"I've been thinking and praying on how to help some of these poor souls who are without food, without medical care, without hope," he intoned. "We can't help them all, at least not yet, but remember the story about the boy who walked along the beach throwing stranded starfishes back into the ocean. We can help some of them, and Love For Africa will be our way to assist them.

"I'm passing around a pamphlet which lays out a plan for helping those desperate people. You'll see it's not a normal situation; we can't just send boxes of food, water, and clothing like we do when there is an emergency nearby. Shipping is costly and slow. Therefore, Peter and I are simply asking for money. Your check will be converted into Somali currency to be used immediately by the people. Friends, I want you to look into your hearts and see how much you are willing to donate to this cause. Peter said he will send photographs of the grateful recipients so you can see for yourselves how their lives are improved."

After he led them in prayers for those suffering around the world, and for the very Earth itself, Jacob Ezel asked two of the attendees (hopefully, the beginning of a congregation) to hand out the pamphlets for his so-called mission. Lauren O'Mooney took a few from Ezel with a nod and a smile; he suddenly felt she could be a tremendous help to him in the future. If only he knew someone was watching him.

"Take two and share one with a friend," he urged them. "The people of Somalia are counting on us to help them. God bless you all."

With service over, everyone left, most of them talking about Love For Africa. A few had their cell phones out, checking the situation in Somalia. Ezel retreated to his office, leaned back in his chair, put his feet up on his desk, and laughed heartily. "You've still got it, Jake," he said out loud. "You deserve an Oscar."

"Yes, you've still got it all right, Jake. I recognized you as soon as I saw you in Dublin. I'm a little surprised you showed up again, but it's been twenty or more years now, so folks probably don't remember you. I couldn't miss you, though, Jake; I wrung a considerable sum out of you when I found you were running a still and bottling the stuff in upscale bottles. You and the wife left town pretty soon afterwards, I recall. Now it appears you're back with another scheme, this time gaming the public as a servant of the Lord. A reverend? Hah! Some folks sure have an ironic sense

of humor. You did balance heartfelt pleas with heartless greed perfectly, I must say. It's an old con, but it still works because people are basically good and kind. Did you hear I died and wasn't a threat anymore? You'd be wrong, and I've got my eye on you." Dean faded away to think.

Jake Ezel was in full swing now. Within two weeks, news about the charismatic reverend who combined beautiful music and powerful biblical messages with a fiery mission to help others living in dire conditions around the world spread like wildfire. Dozens of families would learn about people in African countries like Burundi, South Sudan, and Somalia, who continue to live in poverty despite the abundance of natural resources in their respective countries. Little did his new followers know that when Love For Africa had played out, Plan B - Love For India - would begin shortly thereafter. A mission church was always in need of a good cause.

Jake followed the same pattern: He sang a few of his own songs and a couple of Psalms which he set to music, read passages that focused on doing good deeds and helping those less fortunate, and ended with an update from "Peter Vandeker" on the state of things in Somalia. The pews were more populated this week due to word of mouth advertising and an ad in the weekly newspaper. His coffers began to fill up, too.

For the past two weeks, Lauren O'Mooney had been receiving more and more calls and texts from her assistant in the art gallery asking when she'd be returning, and when they would receive more O'Mooney watercolors. She was torn between her responsibilities as a business owner and adherent of this new church. Pretty soon she'd have to make a decision as, even though she'd started paying for her room at the

Morning Glory, she knew she couldn't stay there forever. She'd had a few conversations with Hayden who seemed more concerned with her sudden church connection than she would have thought. Although she'd always respected his religious convictions, she wished he would support her now in this. What could be a better goal in life than helping others? She'd never really given that much thought before. But, of course, without an income, she wouldn't be able to help as much as she would like. Maybe she should discuss it with Reverend Ezel.

-8-

The Mullen Family

Stacey and Joe Mullen were discussing the new church one evening as they bathed little Paisley and put her to bed. Joe said he had heard in one of his groups that The True Faith church had been steadily growing due to their charismatic new minister. One of his patients, a member of the AA group that met in Joe's office, had even gone to check it out. Joe wondered if the new reverend would provide a meeting room once a week in order to accommodate another group.

"Are you worried about competition with Open Arms, Stacey?" he asked his wife, the former pastor of Open Arms Unitarian Church.

"No, not really. Some people are naturally curious and want to try new things, while others are comfortable with what they have. My worry, if you want to call it that, is there is no permanent pastor at Open Arms. Although I enjoy the Sunday sermons and, frankly, the break Paisley has provided, I've been thinking about going back full-time. Several congregants have told me that as much as they like the temporary pastors, they want me back. Paisley's old enough to be with a sitter when you're not here to watch her, and I'm ready to tackle something more mind-enriching than The Wonky Donkey or Hello, Moon."

"I thought you liked The Wonky Donkey!" Joe said, looking shocked. She elbowed him as they toweled Paisley off and carried her to her crib.

"Well, I have a thought," said Joe. "Why don't we both go to speak with Reverend Ezel? I'll ask about the room, and you can get a feel for his message."

"Hmm," Stacey answered, "good idea. And maybe we won't mention that I'm the pastor at Open Arms, just an interested wife."

"You're not JUST anything, and you know it. But I have to admit, although it's a trifle dishonest, he would probably treat us differently. Being new in town, he might be a little defensive."

"But I am an interested wife, Joe. Do you want to go tomorrow?" she asked. "I could bring Paisley after her nap so she won't be cranky, and you work until one o'clock on Thursdays."

"All right, sounds good," he answered. "I'll give him a call in the morning to make sure he'll be there. If not, we can go another day."

Paisley was now in her pajamas under her light blanket with her stuffed elephant, Fanny. She'd been yawning for a while and said, "Nyny Mommy, nyny Daddy, nyny Fanny." Watching their precious baby drift into sleep confirmed their love and content with this family they had begun.

Joe glanced at his wife as she stifled a yawn.

"It's only eight o'clock," he teased.

"I know, but I've been tired all day. No offense, Joe, but I'm going to turn in early tonight. I can hardly keep my eyes open."

"I understand," he said, kissing her on the cheek. "Paisley is a handful right now. Get a good night's sleep."

-9-

Evolution of a Grifter

Jake was in his office working on a new piece of music when Joe Mullen called the following morning. Jake was gracious and friendly, just the way he liked to come across to potential parishioners, and they made an appointment for two o'clock. Then he went back to his keyboard.

Music was the one thing in his life he was proud of. He played piano and guitar, and had an excellent singing voice. He'd grown up in Miami, Florida, often going to Port of Miami to watch the cruise ships, so when he was eighteen he signed on to one of the lines as a cruise ship musician. The pay and tips were decent, he had free meals and a little room, and his long-term plan was to work his way up to Entertainment Manager one day.

After a year or so, Jake had made friends all around the ship; even the captain came to hear him play and sing once in a while. But Jake had also made friends with one person who would change his life. Yannis Markopoulos was one of several bartenders who worked in the nightclub where Jake performed, therefore Jake saw him in the back of the room three or four times a week. He was a charming Greek, olive-skinned, with a strong nose, hazel eyes, and thick, black hair that he grew to his shoulders. The ladies loved him, of course. Jake noted Yannis's interactions with people thinking he might try that approach with women one day. Still not twenty years old, and very whitebread-looking in comparison to Yannis, he wasn't sure he could pull it off, but it was worth watching and learning.

He and Yannis spoke occasionally as their work schedules allowed, during which time Yannis disclosed his desire in life was to be the next Aristotle Onassis, or at least marry a rich woman. He didn't have the ambition to grow a business, but working on a cruise ship allowed him to meet women, many of whom were wealthy, divorced or widowed. Jake had been surprised when Yannis told him this, but in the end he figured it was just as easily obtained as putting in many years to become Entertainment Manager, maybe easier and faster.

Several years passed and they spoke often about their big dreams and ambitions until one day, out of the blue, Yannis told Jake he was leaving the employ of the cruise ship company as he was getting married.

"Married?" Jake asked, stunned. "I didn't even know you were dating!"

Yannis chuckled. "Yes, Jacob. I shall be marrying a lovely, um, older woman, a recent widow I met on our last cruise. We remained in touch for the past few months, and when she decided to book another cruise to see me again, I was delighted. She actually proposed to me yesterday. I've already turned in my resignation; this shall be my last working cruise. Ah, there she is, my lovely bride to be!"

Jake spun around in the direction Yannis was looking, gasping involuntarily. The woman coming through the doorway was well-dressed and handsome. But she was also many years his senior. Was this the woman? Yes, she smiled at the bartender - it must be her! Walking towards them, she extended her hand to Yannis, then kissed him on the cheek.

Yannis kissed her back gently (he was at work behind the bar, after all), then introduced his friend.

"Mary Louise Griffin, I'd like to introduce my friend, Jacob Ezel. He's a talented musician and good friend of mine."

"Pleased to meet you, ma'am," Jake said, pulling himself together.

"Mr. Ezel, it's nice to meet you in person," she said. "I've seen your show several times; you're a consummate performer."

Jake actually blushed. "Thank you very much," he said. "Yannis told me about your upcoming marriage. Congratulations."

Mary Louise giggled like a girl and locked eyes with her new fiancé. "It was love at first sight for both of us, wasn't it, dear?"

Yannis kissed her hand. "Yes, my love. The moment I laid eyes on you, I knew we were meant to be together."

As Jake restrained a perfunctory smile, his memory flashed back to the many conversations he'd had with his friend about money. When his watch alarm sounded, he shook himself from his reverie and said, "It's time for my next show. It's been a pleasure meeting you, Mrs. Griffin. I'm sure we'll speak again before this cruise is over." Then he turned and walked away.

After his forty-minute performance, Jake looked across the room, but there was another fellow at the bar. Yannis's shift was over and Jake was sure he was with his fiancé, the undoubtedly wealthy Mary Louise. It was late and he was tired, so he went to his little room to chew over the experience and reconsider his goals.

-10-

Business is Booming

In a little under a year of opening, the impact that Fisher Lake Family Park and Campground had made on the city was amazing. Within months, every business in town was booming, and new ones had sprouted up, including two more gas stations, boutiques, gift and specialty shops, and restaurants of all kinds. However, the city's aldermen had rejected all inquiries from the big box stores. Most Dubliners agreed if someone wanted to go to one of those, they could visit another nearby town or city. Dublin wasn't "going corporate"; they preferred home town charm and small family businesses. New homes were also built, and medical facilities increased.

Real estate developer Jason Ford, and entrepreneur Quentin Flatbush, had collaborated on the enlargement of Dublin Middle School in order to build the Dublin High School annex. The high school was a breath of fresh air for the community. Instead of being bused many miles, high-schoolers could walk, bike, drive or hop on the school bus for a few miles. This, in turn, gave them more time to be involved with sports, band, and clubs. Attendance at the Dublin Locomotives ("Locos" for short) football games rose, the community rallied, and the team did very well its first year.

Under construction was the revitalization of Dublin's old train station, including an actual steam engine with a gift shop car and two dining cars that served elegant meals in the manner of trains from the turn of the twentieth century. It was due to open within the next few months. Joel Turner was especially proud of this project, as he had found the old steam train for sale, purchased it for the city, had it transported to Dublin, and steered the construction process. Joel had his fingers crossed it would become a good tourist draw. After all, Dublin had been established to accommodate railroad workers since the 1890s, and was an important stop on the line which ran from the east coast, stretching through Tennessee and to the west. "The Old Train Station" would be interesting for tourists, and provide a unique dining experience for everyone.

But nothing topped the campground as a destination. Just a week after opening to five-star reviews, it was booked solid for six weeks and online reservations continued steadily. Owner Barbara Scanlan and developer Jason Ford had become engaged but could find no time to plan a big wedding, so Pastor Stacey Mullen had the pleasure of marrying them the day after Thanksgiving with a small group of attendees; they promised to do it up right later on.

Dean smiled as he floated around town one lovely day with Janet, his also-deceased wife. Of all the wonderful places they had visited since having the option to travel anywhere they wished, it sometimes surprised them that this little town of around fifteen thousand residents (and growing) pulled on them so.

"Home is where your heart is," Janet had noted once.

"That may be true, my dear," answered Dean, "since your heart is buried next to mine in the family plot."

Janet's spirit glowed with laughter as she swatted at him. "Anyway, when I realize how much you had to lose in order for all this to happen, I'm very proud of you," she said.

"I lost nothing by doing the right thing in the end," Dean replied. "In fact, it was the opposite. Hey, let's go visit Hayden at the B&B. I smell charcoal burning. Wonder what's for supper? Oh, I know we don't eat; we can't eat. But sometimes, when I'm around a good meal, memory serves me well."

Janet just laughed at him as they floated away.

-11-

The Morning Glory Felines

On this warm Saturday morning, two young cats lay in the sunbeams that filtered through their special catio at The Morning Glory B&B. One was a calico, fastidiously washing her paws. The other, a tuxedo black, lay on his back enjoying the warmth of this spring morning. As they lounged, the catio door opened and a child entered carrying two bowls of cat food. Breakfast had arrived along with their favorite person, Ellie Monroe.

"Good morning, kitties," she sang out. "Are you hungry this morning?"

They answered with meows, and purred loudly, weaving themselves between her legs.

Ellie smiled at them. "I think you need a brushing, Mr. Oreo. Have you been rolling in the dirt again?"

The black and white cat murmured in reply as he crunched his kibble.

"And Callie, you look very beautiful this morning. Your coat is so shiny."

The calico raised her head out of her food bowl and mewed her appreciation.

Ellie laughed. "I wish I could understand what you say to me. Maybe someday I'll learn how to speak cat".

After they'd finished eating, Ellie reached for the cat brush. "Come on, Oreo. You'll look nicer for the guests when your fur is clean."

Ellie was not yet eight years old. She had saved these kittens eighteen months ago by bringing them to the B&B in a cardboard box, requesting the owners to give them a home before her father took them to the forest to fend for themselves. Hayden and Fiona had brought them in and cared for them, even adding the catio as part of the building's renovation. Several weeks after dropping them off, Ellie had cautiously knocked on the front door asking to see the kittens. One thing led to another and, after receiving a letter of consent from her mother, Ellie was given the title of Senior Cat Wrangler. Her job was to take care of the animals, feeding and brushing them, and cleaning their litter boxes.

The sibling cats held what they felt was an important and exalted position in the B&B. After all, they were catered to all day by their servants. When they wanted attention, they entered the solarium via a cat flap and walked around the place like they owned it, enjoying the attention and affection of the tourists and staff. They were not allowed in the kitchen, but were rewarded for their patience with a little chicken or fish on their cat food at night. And when they needed solitude, back into the catio they would go where nobody but they (and their servants) could enter.

After Ellie was finished with her chores, she spent a few minutes talking to the cats. A new visitor saw her and knocked on the glass to get her attention. Ellie left the catio and entered the solarium.

"Hello," she said to the woman.

"Hello," the woman answered. "Do you live here?"

"No, I work here," Ellie answered with pride. "I'm the Senior Cat Wrangler."

"Oh, that's very nice," the woman said, bemused. "Well, I was wondering if you might help me out. You see, my son Lucas loves cats. We had one for a little while, but it ran off and Lucas has been unhappy since that happened. When I saw your kitties, I thought maybe it would be okay if he could visit with them while we stay here."

"Sure, Mrs. - uh, what's your name? Mine is Ellie."

"Oh, I'm sorry. I'm Mrs. Nunez. We're in the Petunia Suite for the week."

Ellie made a mental note of this information. Her cats were important to her, and she felt a great deal of responsibility for them.

"If Lucas comes to the solarium, Callie and Oreo will come out to meet him. They like making friends."

"Ellie, I have to tell you Lucas uses a wheelchair to get around. Would it scare them?"

At that moment, Fiona entered the solarium with a small flowerpot in her hands and saw Ellie speaking with one of the new visitors. "Oh, hello, sorry to interrupt. I'm Fiona O'Mooney."

"I'm Rachel Nunez," the woman answered. "We spoke on the phone a few days ago. My son and I arrived last night. I was just speaking with your Senior Cat Wrangler here who told me the cats might like to meet Lucas."

Fiona remembered the phone call regarding the child who was confined to his wheelchair, requiring concessions to the usual schedule.

"Of course I remember," she said. "Yes, our cats thrive on attention; I'm pretty sure they think it's their job."

"Thank you both," Mrs. Nunez said with a smile. "Lucas is asleep right now; yesterday was a long ride. Perhaps he could visit with them after lunch. I also want to take him through the beautiful gardens I saw through our window. We'll see you later!" Then she turned and walked away, waving goodbye.

Fiona said, "Well, Miss Ellie Monroe, Curly Pete grew some catnip for the kitties, wasn't that nice? Let's put it in the catio where they can enjoy it. And if you're done here for now, why don't you wash up, because he also told me there are some chocolate chip muffins left from breakfast that will go stale by afternoon if they're not eaten pretty soon. And it's payday, too."

Ellie smiled and nodded. She was paid two dollars a day for taking care of the cats Monday through Saturday. That was pretty good for an almost-eight-year-old. Fiona didn't know Ellie gave the money to her mother because her father had lost his job. For now, she was the breadwinner of the family.

-12-

The Little Breadwinner

Dean Brennan had dropped by the B&B to see what his son, Hayden, was up to. He hadn't known about Hayden's existence until the day of his own fatal heart attack. But now he had the opportunity to watch Hayden run The Morning Glory and paint his beautiful watercolors. He was also happy his former assistant, Fiona, had married Hayden. When Dean noticed Ellie talking with Fiona he thought, *Ellie Monroe? I wonder if she's one of Trey Monroe's brood? Not to be uncharitable, but the one thing Monroe does best is to help his wife conceive. I should drop by the house and see if I'm thinking of the same fellow. Not that I'm nosy, not at all. It's for the child's sake.* And Dean Brennan poofed himself out of The Morning Glory.

In a moment, Dean was outside a run-down clapboard house, once painted blue and white, a half-mile from the B&B, close to the unused railroad spur. He watched several young children in the front yard playing noisily with worn-out toys. An American flag nailed to the porch waved wistfully in the breeze, its days of glory gone to tatters, colors faded by the sun. Someone had planted zinnias in a small flower bed under the front window, their bold hot-palate colors drawing the eye away from the house's faded paint. When Dean saw Ellie walking up the dirt road, his ghostly heart fluttered. Lost in thought, she walked past him, took the ten-dollar bill and two ones from her pants pocket, said hello to her siblings, and entered the house. Dean followed.

The inside of the house was no better than the outside, although there were some touches of color here and there as if a person with perhaps five minutes to herself needed something cheerful to look at.

"Momma, I'm home!" Ellie sang out.

"Hush, Ellie!" the woman said, hurrying out of the kitchen. "Don't holler, you'll wake your father." But then, realizing she was scolding the child, she took her in her arms and hugged her. "How are the kitties today?"

"They're fine, Momma. And here's my pay," she said, proudly holding out the bills.

"You should keep this, Ellie; you worked for it," her mother whispered.

"Huh, uh, I won't. I want you to have it," the little girl insisted. "I don't need anything."

Mrs. Monroe sighed. How did this happen, she asked herself for the hundredth time. My child and husband have switched places. "Thank you, Ellie," she said. "You're my sweetheart." She hugged the child close again.

I was right, Dean thought.

At that moment, Trey stumbled out of the bedroom looking as ragged and faded as the flag hanging outside. "Hey, Ellie, did you get your pay?" he asked.

No "good morning" or "how are you", Dean fumed, as Mrs. Monroe and Ellie stared at their feet wordlessly.

"Well?" Trey repeated, holding out his hand.

Mrs. Monroe spoke up quietly. "Trey, I need to buy food for the children. I can't give you the money this time."

Taking a few steps towards his wife, he threatened, "I'm the man of the house, Amanda - gimme that money!"

He raised his arm as if to strike, but it became frozen in the air as if someone was holding it tightly. Ellie and her mother watched in fascinated horror as he struggled to loosen himself. Trey cursed, then cried. This must be the end of him, he thought - the result of self-pity and alcohol. The grip on his arm finally relaxed and Trey slumped to the floor. In his ear he heard, "You've hit the bottom, Monroe, and now you have two choices - die or get help. You dug the hole so it's up to you to climb out of it."

Amanda instinctively took a step forward to assist her husband, but Ellie put her arm out to stop her. "Leave him be, Momma. You can't help him. Daddy needs to fix himself. That's what the angel said."

Stunned by the child's words, Amanda backed off, leaving Trey on the floor.

Trey Monroe lay there for a long time after the voice left. He didn't want to die, but he didn't know where to find help. Fired from the best job he'd ever had, he'd turned to the bottle for solace and just look where it got him. He knew he was as powerless over alcohol as his parents had been. Sniffling and stuffed with tears, he rolled onto his back and stared at the ceiling. "Somebody please help me," he whispered. "I don't know how."

I watched the man lying on the floor for several minutes. Well, I didn't know I could do that. But then again, I never tried. I had to die in order to turn my life around. I hope this was enough of an incentive for Monroe to do the same. Then Dean poofed himself away; it was time to return to The Great Beyond and his beloved wife, Janet.

-13-

Goings-on at the B&B

"Mom, can you help me put my shoes and socks on?"

"I'll be right there, Lucas," was the reply. Rachel Nunez set her lipstick case down and entered the bedroom of the Petunia Suite where her son was holding a bright red pair of socks.

"I want to wear these with my red sneakers," he said. "I think the cats will like them."

Rachel smiled at him. "I'm sure they will. Cats can see colors, although they see them differently than we do. Remember that TV show, 'Cat Fanciers'?"

"Yeah, that's a cool show," Lucas answered, then paused. "I wish I had a cat."

"Let's get you well first," his mother said, "so you can take care of a cat."

"Promise?"

"Yes, I promise. So, let's get these socks and shoes on, then go downstairs to meet the bed and breakfast cats."

A few minutes later, as the elevator S-L-O-W-L-Y descended to the first floor, Lucas sighed. "This is no Disney World ride, is it, Mom?"

"No," she smiled, remembering their recent visit to Orlando, "but I think it only seems longer when you're looking forward to something fun. Or if you're hungry."

"Or both!" Lucas exclaimed.

"Well, how about we have lunch with the owners, visit with the cats, then tour the beautiful garden. Tomorrow morning we'll go to the campground - is that a good plan?"

The elevator finally stopped and the door slid open behind the reception desk. Receptionist Rosemary Zimmer turned in her chair and smiled at the Nunezes. She felt sorry for the young boy in a wheelchair, but he was all smiles.

Rosemary beamed back, then asked Rachel, "Is everything okay with your suite? Do you need anything?"

"My goodness!" Rachel chuckled. "It's the most beautiful suite I've ever stayed in, and there is nothing more we need. You've thought of everything."

"Thanks, that's good news. Have a great day," Rosemary said as she turned to answer the phone.

There were only two people in the dining room; most of the visitors were out shopping, visiting the campground, or driving around sightseeing in the area, as they were on their own after breakfast. But due to Lucas's wheelchair which made transport a challenge, they had been invited to eat with the O'Mooneys until suitable transportation could be arranged for the following day, the day they were to visit the . Fiona and Hayden were seated in the dining room at one of the tables, and waved Rachel and Lucas over.

"Hi, there," Hayden said as he stood up. "I haven't had the opportunity to meet you yet, but I'm Hayden O'Mooney. My wife, Fiona, told me you'd arrived."

Rachel smiled, pushed Lucas's wheelchair up to the table and sat next to him. She said, "After lunch we're going to visit your cats. Is your Senior Cat Wrangler around?"

"No, I'm sorry," Fiona answered. "Ellie comes in the morning and late afternoon to feed and spend some quality time with Callie and Oreo. But I'm free, if you like."

"May I pet them?" Lucas broke in.

"Sure, they're very friendly."

"I hope they're not scared of this stupid wheelchair," Lucas grumbled. "Or this giant leg cast."

"I think they'll be okay with it," Fiona answered with a reassuring smile.

While the others were talking about the cats, Hayden had gone into the kitchen to confer with Curly Pete. He came back to announce that lunch would be a choice of grilled cheese and bacon sandwich and homemade tomato soup, or mushroom quiche with a fruit cup. And for dessert, there were giant blueberry muffins from Mom's Bakery. Lucas spoke up first, since he was "starving". He asked for the grilled cheese sandwich and soup. Rachel and Fiona requested quiche.

"Okay, grilled cheese for the guys, quiche for the girls," Hayden said, and went back into the kitchen.

Suddenly, there was a flash of lightning and a terrifying crack of thunder.

"Wow, that was close!" Fiona exclaimed, quickly turning to look out the window. When she turned back around, she saw Rachel comforting her trembling son, while heavy rain began to pummel the window.

"It's okay, honey, it's okay," she crooned to Lucas who had become white as a sheet.

Fiona didn't know what to say or do, so she sat quietly until Hayden returned.

"That was some noise, wasn't it? It must have hit very close," he said.

"Yes," Rachel whispered. "If it's all right with you, we're going back upstairs. Lucas needs to rest."

"Of course!" Fiona said immediately. "Shall we bring your lunches to your room?"

Rachel nodded to Fiona as she wheeled Lucas from the table. "That's very kind of you, thanks."

Hayden and Fiona sat quietly for a minute, watching Mrs. Nunez push her son's wheelchair into the lobby.

"I wonder what happened?" Hayden said. "Did the lightning scare him?"

Fiona nodded. "I think so. He was fine up until then. I hope he'll be okay."

"Well, I'm going to have lunch then go outside to see if there's any damage. That bolt of lightning was too close for comfort," said Hayden, as the heavy rain continued to beat the dining room windows with loud plops.

The Nunezes remained in their suite for the rest of the day.

In the morning when Ellie arrived at the Morning Glory, she wiped her shoes on the mat and stepped into the kitchen. She waved at Izzy as he set the breakfast plates and cutlery onto a rolling cart.

"Good morning, Izzy!" she sang out. "Did you see that big tree that fell across the driveway?"

"Sure did," he replied with a big nod of his head. "A lightning bolt hit it, then it fell on Miss Lauren's rental car, squashed the top right in. The boss asked if I knew someone with a chainsaw and I told him I have a cousin who's a handyman; he'll be here pretty soon to cut it up and haul it away. Did you have breakfast yet? Mom's Bakery just delivered cinnamon buns."

Ellie was tempted, but she knew the buns were for guests first; those were the rules. "Well, if there's one left after the guests are done, maybe I can have one before school starts." Secretly, she hoped a few guests were allergic to cinnamon.

On her way to the catio, Ellie overheard two people talking loudly in the back hallway.

"But Hayden," she heard, "How am I supposed to go to church today? Why can't I borrow your car this morning?"

"Because I need it to run some errands, Lauren. Why are you so invested in this church all of a sudden?

"I'm not sure," Lauren admitted. "Maybe for the first time in my life, I feel a sense of purpose. This project is vital and the reverent needs my help. I have the time, so why not?"

"Speaking of which, I thought you came here to talk about the art gallery with me, get more artwork, and work out a contract or something; but we really haven't sat down together. What's going on?"

"Am I wearing out my welcome, Hayden?" she asked, wide-eyed. "I can pay for the suite, if that's what you're implying."

"No, of course not," Hayden answered. "It's just ..."

Now, Ellie needed to tend to the cats and go to school. She didn't have time to wait for Hayden and Lauren to finish their conversation, so she decided to make a little noise to let them know someone was there. She dropped her book bag on the floor and said "Oops!", which had the effect she was hoping for. Hayden and Lauren stopped talking and turned in her direction.

"Good morning, Ellie," said Hayden. "On your way to feed the kitties?"

"Yes," she answered, "but I'm sorry to interrupt your conversation."

"It's all right, sweetie, Lauren assured her. "I think we were done talking for now anyway, weren't we, Hayden?"

"I suppose so," he answered. "Izzy's cousin is coming soon to cut up the tree and haul it away, and you need to contact the rental company about giving you another car. We can finish our discussion later."

Uh-oh, looks like I have to figure out how to keep Hayden's ex-wife away from Jake. She seems interested in his so-called church mission, and she'll be hurt if he gets ahold of her wallet. Would I feel this way if Hayden wasn't my own son? I'd certainly like to think so. And Dean poofed away to give the situation a little thought.

-14-

The Accident

Lucas Nunez was eleven years old, and up until five months ago, he lived a normal life. His mother was a school dietician in Decatur, Alabama, where they lived. His father was always busy, but took him places on the weekends, just the two guys together. Often, they went to "the office", but that was fine. Dad's office was pretty cool because he worked at the U.S. Space and Rocket Center in Huntsville. Lucas learned about space travel and exploration just from meandering around the museum with and without his father. He'd gone to Space Camp since he was nine, but this summer he wouldn't be going.

It had been an ordinary spring morning. Lucas was looking forward to going to Huntsville that day because he would get a sneak peek at a new exhibition, one that wouldn't be open to the public for another week. After breakfast and a hug and kiss from Mom, the two guys started out. It was a little cloudy and there was rain in the forecast, but the car was new and comfortable. Tomas Nunez inserted their favorite CD and they sang along with it for fifteen minutes until it started to rain. No, it wasn't rain - it was a cascade. All of a sudden, Tomas couldn't see too far in front of the car, so he slowed down, staying in the right lane. They drove on, carefully following the cars ahead, until a bolt of lightning hit a tree on their side of the street, and there was a terrifying electrical crack. Tomas tried to stop in time to avoid the tree as it fell onto the street, but it landed on the hood. Then everything began happening at once - the airbags inflated, mashing Lucas into the seat; a car

58

traveling too closely slammed into the back of theirs, and a tree limb rammed the passenger side of the car.

Lucas gasped for the air that had been knocked out of him, and as he gathered his wits, he realized he was trapped. Panicking, he called for his father, but there was no answer. Tomas was still sitting straight up in his seat, but his head had fallen to one side.

"Dad! Dad!" Lucas cried out. He tried to touch his father, but his seatbelt kept him from reaching far enough, and he couldn't move his right leg for leverage.

A man ran to the car, followed by three more, to help them out. Someone called 9-1-1 and two ambulances and two fire trucks arrived in a few minutes. Lucas was in shock - eyes open but unseeing, unable to speak.

Lucas was transported to Huntsville Hospital for Women and Children which specialized in advanced pediatrics. Tomas was transported to Huntsville Hospital. It took a crew over an hour to move the fallen tree off the road, tow the vehicles away, and get traffic back to normal. Consequently, after a phone call from the Huntsville Police directing her to Women and Children's Hospital, Rachel Nunez's panicked drive there was twice as long as she expected. By the time she arrived, found a parking spot, and ran into the emergency room, she was an emotional wreck. Two hospital volunteers helped calm her down, ascertained the situation, and turned her over to an emergency room nurse who briefly explained the situation to her.

Rachel was finally allowed to be with her son in his cubicle. He was asleep with tubes in his arms and an oxygen tube in his nostrils. A heart monitor beeped loudly beside the bed.

In less than a minute, the ER physician entered the cubicle and introduced himself. He told Rachel her son's right hip and femur had been badly broken. Lucas would have to undergo surgery to reset the bones, then wear a hip-to-foot cast until they healed. Lucas had also sustained a broken rib from the airbag, but that required no intervention except for bandaging.

"And my husband? Where is my husband?" She looked quickly around the ER for clues as to his whereabouts. "Is he here?"

The physician hated this part of the job. His duty was to heal, but sometimes the outcome was out of his hands. He looked Rachel in the eye as he softly said, "Mrs. Nunez, your husband was killed in the accident. He died at the scene."

Rachel shook her head and cried, "No, no, no, no! That can't be true! Let me see him, please take me to him!" She turned to look for Tomas, but the doctor caught her shoulders and stopped her.

"He isn't in the ER, Mrs. Nunez. If you will wait in this chair, I'll get someone to discuss the situation with you. Will you please sit here for a moment?"

Unable to think, Rachel sat on the chair, crying. In a moment, a young woman walked in with a box of tissues and offered them to her, saying in a calm, quiet voice, "Mrs. Nunez, my name is Claudia Meadows, one of the social workers here. I'm very sorry about the loss of your husband. I know this is a tremendous shock for you."

Rachel sobbed into her hands. Her husband was dead, her son needed surgery. What had started as a fun day for the guys had turned into a horrible nightmare. She didn't know what to do next; she felt drained and confused. She wanted to stand but her legs felt weak and useless.

"Is there something I can do for you right now,?" the social worker asked gently.

In a cracking voice, Rachel answered, "Just tell me what I'm supposed to do next. Do I go to my son or to my husband?"

"There is nothing we can do for your husband now. I suggest you stay with your son until surgery is arranged, then we'll go from there, one step at a time. Is that okay with you?"

Rachel nodded, wiped her eyes and blew her nose. Ms. Meadows handed her the box of tissues and led her back to Lucas's cubicle. Then she brought Rachel a cup of water and said she would stay with her for a while.

"Thank you," Rachel whispered, watching her son's even breathing. She knew she had to remain strong to face the future, whatever that might be.

Hours later, someone roused Rachel from a light sleep in the OR waiting room. The surgeon, still wearing her surgical cap, said, "Mrs. Nunez, I'm Dr. Simms. We just finished Lucas's surgery, and he did very well. He's going to be fine."

Rachel was wide awake. "Gracias a Dios!" she exclaimed while making the sign of the cross. "When can I see him?"

"He's being taken to recovery, then he'll be admitted to a room. Wait right here and a volunteer will show you to the recovery area," Dr. Simms answered.

"Thank you, thank you so much," Rachel said with relief. Her son would be fine in time, she knew. How much time she couldn't guess, but that wasn't an issue just now. She closed her eyes and gave thanks for the good doctors and hospital staff who helped Lucas. Her beloved Tomas was gone, and she would grieve for and miss him always, but Lucas was alive; now she would be both his mother and father to the best of her ability.

-15-

First Day at the Campground

The morning after his meltdown in the dining room, the sky was clear and sunny - and Lucas was hungry.

Once more, Rachel Nunez brought her son to the lobby. When they passed the reception desk, they said good morning to Rosemary and headed for the dining room, where they found Fiona.

"Good morning to you both," she said cheerily. "Are you feeling better this morning?"

"Yes, thank you," Rachel said. "We're grateful the storm didn't last too long. Lucas is looking forward to visiting the campground today."

"Yeah," he added. "I want to see everything, but most of all the farm animals and their babies."

"He's read the pamphlet several times," Rachel explained, "and has it all planned out."

"That's wonderful," said Fiona with a smile. "Jason Ford, who helped develop the campground, will be here at 8:30 to pick you up, so make sure you eat a good breakfast to keep you going for a while. Please join our other guests, and if you need anything special, just ask me."

"Are there waffles?" Lucas asked.

"Yep, you make them yourself. Or rather, your mom can make you one. It's fun and there are lots of toppings."

"What are we waiting for, Mom? I'm starving!"

"You're always starving," Rachel laughed. "Okay, let's go and we can meet the other guests, too."

"Before we leave, I want to see the cats, " Lucas reminded his mother. "I've been waiting for a couple of days."

"You're in luck then," said Fiona. "Ellie just got here. You might catch her before she goes to school in about thirty minutes."

"Okay, thanks!" said Lucas. "Mom, can we hurry?"

The waffles were fun to make and delicious. Lucas asked his mother to top them with whipped cream and strawberries. When they finished, Rachel said, "Hold onto your hat," and whipped the wheelchair away towards the solarium.

The room was sunny and warm. Rachel saw Ellie in the catio and waved to her.

"I'll be right there!" Ellie hollered. She disinfected her hands and entered the solarium. She had never seen a wheelchair before and gave it a quick assessment. Then she said to Lucas, "Hi, I'm Ellie. Are you here to see the kitties?"

"Yes, please," Lucas answered eagerly.

Ellie went back into the catio and unlatched the cat door to the solarium. Callie and Oreo ran out and stopped when they saw the wheelchair.

"Oh," Lucas said sadly. "I was afraid of that. The wheelchair scares them."

"No, it's just something new. They've never seen one before. Give them a minute."

And before Ellie finished the sentence Callie jumped into Lucas's lap, purring and rubbing her soft face on Lucas's t-shirt. Oreo walked around the wheelchair, sniffing it until he decided it was safe, then he joined his sister. Lucas was ecstatic. Both cats were purring loudly and Rachel smiled from ear to ear.

"They like me!" Lucas exclaimed. "What are their names?"

"The calico girl is Callie, and the black and white boy is Oreo."

"Are they your kitties?" asked Rachel.

"Not really. I brought them here to save them, and they're very happy now. Everybody loves them - well, except for Miss Lauren who doesn't like cat hair on her clothes."

Fiona walked into the solarium to remind Ellie it was getting late. "I've got to run a few errands this morning, so I'd be happy to drop you off at school. Oh, and there are two cinnamon buns left, if you're interested."

"Yes, please, Miss Fiona. I don't want to be late, and I definitely would like a bun."

"Then I'll meet you in the foyer in a few minutes," Fiona said.

Ellie turned to Lucas. "They'll hop down pretty soon, or you can tell them 'down'. I'll see you later," she said, then walked quickly away to the kitchen to grab her backpack and cinnamon buns.

"What a sweet child," Rachel commented to Fiona.

"Yes, she's a very special child, and precocious," Fiona agreed, then looked at her watch. "I need to get going. Jason should be here in twenty minutes. Is there anything you need to do before he gets here?"

"I guess we should brush our teeth," Rachel answered. "Lucas was packed and ready to go before we went to bed last night. We'll be back in just a few minutes."

Lucas just grinned as his mother pushed his wheelchair towards the elevator.

As Fiona entered the kitchen area, she heard the sound of a chainsaw, and stepped outside to see. Two men were cutting off big tree limbs, and hauling them into an open trailer. She looked at the tree, split in two and charred at the top, lying across Lauren's rental car and the driveway.

As she stood there wondering how long the tree had stood there, Hayden walked over and put his arm around her waist, reading her thoughts. "That oak tree was about two hundred years old," he said. "The guys counted the rings. I asked them if they could leave the stump. The roots are still intact and digging it out would leave a huge crater. Maybe we can do something with the stump in the future."

Fiona nodded. She saw no need to uproot the remains of the old oak either. Then she waved to Jason as he pulled up with a wheelchair accessible van. Jason greeted them and extended the ramp.

From the foyer, Rachel saw Jason pull up and wheeled Lucas outside. "Good morning, Mr. Ford. I'm Rachel Nunez and this is my son, Lucas. What a lovely van," she said with a smile.

"Thank you," said Jason. "I think it will do the trick."

But Rachel had her eyes on the sky as she said, "It's clouding up. Is it supposed to rain?" she asked, fearing another incident with thunder and lightning, and she hesitated to push the wheelchair up to the ramp. She could see Lucas was nervous; he had lost his excitement for visiting the campground and hadn't said a word although he'd been chattering non-stop about this since he woke up. A light breeze wafted over.

Jason said, "According to the weatherman this morning, we might get scattered showers on and off, but there are plenty of buildings and shelters to duck into. And since I helped plan the campground , I know where all those places are," he added helpfully.

"It's not the rain that I'm concerned about, but thunderstorms in particular," Rachel said quietly.

Hayden and Fiona had joined them at the van and understood Rachel's concern. Fiona laid her hand on Rachel's arm. "You'll be here for three more days. You could put it off," she offered.

Lucas finally spoke up. "Heck, no! I've been looking forward to this for a long time, and I'm going." He looked at his mother with pleading eyes. "We are going, aren't we, Mom? I can only get over my fear by facing it - that's what the doctor said."

The adults in attendance gaped at the boy, who turned his wheelchair back towards the ramp with conviction. "Mom?"

Minutes later, they were on their way.

Jason Ford was true to his word. He ushered the Nunezes around the campground with efficiency and maximum comfort. They planned to see half of it today and the rest tomorrow. Beginning with the farmhouse, corrals, and barn where the baby animals were kept, they moved to the farmyard to feed the goats and alpacas which Lucas enjoyed. He was also very interested in how a farm runs and everything it involved.

"It's complicated," he said to his mother. "I always thought farming was pretty easy, but it's definitely not."

Rachel laughed. "It's a lot of hard work, Lucas. My grandparents were farmers in Mexico. You have to be very smart, physically fit, and strong-willed to run a farm."

"That's true," Jason added. "Well, what would you like to see next, Lucas?"

"Can we go to the lake to watch the boats?"

"Sure we can. Let's get back in the van and we'll drive over there. I'll show you the canoe and kayak rentals, then the sailboat rentals and the paddle boats. Then it might be time to grab something to eat. How does that sound?"

After a ninety-minute lake tour, as they were sitting at a refreshment stand with a cool drink, Rachel said she was very tired. "That was a lot of walking, Mr. Ford. I'm glad I wore my most comfortable sneakers."

"Uh, oh, Lucas," said Jason with a wink. "I think you wore your mother out. Why don't we head back to the B&B where you can get some rest?"

"Okay," Lucas agreed. "But we are coming back tomorrow, right?"

"Yes, you'll be here, but you'll have another guide. I have some business to attend to, so I've spoken with one of our staff, Trey Monroe. He had a lot to do with building the trails. He's a native of the area, so he can answer any questions you have. I've already arranged for Izzy Morningsong from the B&B to bring you here at 9:00 and take you home at 2:00. How does that sound?"

"Wonderful," Rachel answered. "We know Izzy, and we appreciate all the extra assistance you and the Morning Glory B&B have provided us."

Lucas bounced and wiggled as much as his cast allowed. "I can't wait to go on that special nature trail and spot some deer, coyotes and skunks."

"Um, maybe not coyotes and skunks, Lucas, but deer are likely," Jason said with a smile.

Lucas yawned. "I am pretty tired," he admitted.

"Too much fresh air," Rachel said.

"And I'm also still hungry!"

"Come on, Lucas, we'll get you a corn dog. That should hold you until you get back to The Morning Glory," Jason laughed.

-16-

The Trip to Cherokee

Three weeks after the family met at The Golden Goblet Tavern, twenty members of the Morningsong family left for Cherokee, NC. Barney drove his mother, Awinita, and step-father, Enoli, in his car. Tallulah drove her cousin, Curly Pete, and his brother, Bald Cypress or "BC". Marvin Miller, a mechanic at Flatbush Gas & Auto Repair, had married into the Morningsong family when he wed Grace ten years prior. He had an older, but reliable, mini bus in which he brought more relatives from Dublin and a couple of surrounding towns.

The two-hour caravan went quickly as everybody admired the beautiful Smoky Mountains scenery, and it wasn't until they reached the sign reading "Welcome to Cherokee Indian Reservation" that Barney felt his heart swell. They were about to meet with the Principal Chief and the Tribal Council of the Eastern Band of Cherokee Indians, itself being a sovereign nation with its own laws, elections, government, and institutions.

Enoli, silent since they left home, asked Barney, "Is the Principal Chief's position comparable to the President of the United States? I've never been clear on this. It's a country within a country, is it not?"

As Barney drove past another sign reading "Welcome To Our Nation" he said, "I don't know, Stepfather. I've never thought about that."

"I will ask him," Enoli returned, nodding his head, falling silent once more.

Barney's mother smiled. "My husband is a quiet man, but his few words are thoughtful."

The caravan drove through the reservation to their motel where they parked their vehicles and met in the parking lot, forming a circle around Barney's car.

"Our meeting is in two hours," he said to everyone. "Mother, Father, Tallulah, Wally Brown Bear, Curly Pete and I will speak with the Principal Chief to reiterate our agenda. Shortly after, we will all convene with the tribal leaders. I suggest we get settled into our rooms, have some lunch, then rest or look around a little until then. Is that okay?"

"Which way is the casino?" a voice called out, followed by some laughter amongst the crowd.

"Oh, no you don't, Charlie Kawonu!" old Mrs. Morningsong said, louder than anyone had heard her before. "If you disappear, I will tell your wife and all her relatives."

Charlie hung his head as one of his friends whispered in his ear, "Don't joke with Grandmother. She may be tiny, but she means what she says. Don't forget, she's the granddaughter of Chief Truth-Teller."

"I meant no disrespect, Grandmother. I promised my wife I would stay away from the casino, and I will keep my promise. I only made a joke."

Awinita nodded, then turned to her granddaughter. "Tallulah, I would like to eat, then rest before meeting with the Principal Chief. I see a diner across the road that promises authentic Cherokee dining. Will you go with me? I would love a bowl of succotash if they have it."

"Of course, Grandmother," answered Tallulah. "I'd be happy to."

"Me, too," said Barney; Enoli, Curly Pete and Wally Brown Bear also chimed in. "What a treat to just sit and eat without having to prepare the food and clean up later," Barney added.

"Nobody makes fry bread like Awinita," Enoli said quietly, as usual.

Blushing like a young woman with the compliment, she thanked him.

After eating, they returned to their motel rooms for a short nap, then freshened up for their meeting. Barney checked at least three times that the documents found at The Morning Glory B&B during its renovation were in his briefcase. "I'm not sure why I'm so nervous," he said to Tallulah. "I know they'll guide us with wisdom."

When the Dublin contingent presented themselves at the government building, they were ushered into a large reception area, then taken to a large meeting room with a round table where sat the Principal Chief. He stood, said "O si yo", and held out his hand to greet them all. In deference to their age, he pulled out chairs closest to his own for Awinita and Enoli.

When everyone was seated, he said, "It's good to meet you all. I had the pleasure of meeting Awinita Morningsong many years ago. Do you remember, kinswoman?"

Awinita smiled shyly. "I do remember. After the death of my second husband, I traveled here with two women friends to seek your advice about marrying for a third time. Although you were quite young at the time, Chief, you were already wise and provided an answer I was happy to hear."

"Grandmother?" Tallulah blurted out. "I - we - had no idea you've already been to Cherokee. All of us thought you went to visit relatives."

"I <u>was</u> visiting relatives. The Chief and I are cousins through Truth-Teller's maternal line."

The crowd gasped in awe. The stories were true.

The Chief smiled. "It's been too long, cousin. You knew the door was always open to you."

"I have been happy with my life since that meeting," she said with a smile. "However, we now have a puzzle to solve that requires assistance from those with a higher authority." And with that, she handed over the documents they had brought with them.

The Principal Chief looked them over, raising his eyebrows several times. When he was done, he said, "These are very important documents. Clearly, an injustice was committed over a hundred years ago which should be rectified in some way. I'm not a lawyer, but it appears that thousands of acres of land were stolen from the Cherokee in your area. We'll discuss all of this with the council in a few minutes and hear what they have to say."

An assistant was asked to bring in the Vice Chief and Tribal Council, then the Principal Chief said, "It will take a few minutes for the members to arrive. In the meantime, stretch, relax, and above all, don't worry. We've settled a few similar cases in the past which benefited everyone concerned."

Members of the Tribal Council began entering and introducing themselves. The Vice Chief plus nine women and men represented every important faction of the Nation of The Eastern Band of Cherokee Indians, such as Education, Finance, Police, Agriculture, Housing, and so on. The Dubliners were impressed with their professional demeanor and interest, and felt the outcome of their decisions would be satisfactory and just.

After everyone was seated, copies of the documents dated 1878 and 1879 were handed around the table.

The Principal Chief began. "Speaking for everyone present - even those of you who haven't had the opportunity to read through these papers completely - I am once again appalled by the greed and corruption evident here." Tapping the papers with his finger, he added, "It's an old story, but one we have dealt with before. I'll give everyone a few minutes to read through this material."

The Dublin Cherokee were not impatient, and waited quietly. They had all heard Barney relate the story in The Golden Goblet - how the intercontinental railway spurs had grown, bringing immigrant labor with them; how it irked the Cherokee who felt the land was merely on loan to them while they occupied and cared for it; how the original deed and lawsuit were discovered in The Morning Glory B&B; how the Cherokee retaliated and sent the settlers packing; and how the Cherokee were finally given back their land by the Bureau of Indian Affairs. Now they waited to hear what the Principal Chief, Vice Chief, and Tribal Council would say. When the Tribal Council members finished reading, the Principal Chief spoke again.

"Friends, it's patently clear that Mr. Worthington took advantage of the Cherokee living in the area of Dublin, TN, and surrounding areas, in order to build a logging empire for himself, and was supported in his claim by the questionable Commissioner Nicholson, who spoke out of both sides of his mouth. Although the land was returned to the Cherokee, the issue is that years later, the land was once again sold without the permission of its legal inhabitants. Have I understood this correctly?" he asked.

Barney spoke up. "This is more of a statement, not a question. We have considered several options for this land, but they aren't punitive. For instance, the house that was not destroyed is now a bed and breakfast, bringing money into the city. Several of our kinsmen work there for good wages. Whatever the conclusion is, we prefer it protects the remaining woodlands and the lake and river that run through it. So far, development there has been conservative, although the lake is now being used for recreational purposes, and it borders the woodlands."

"It appears you favor a peaceful approach, and request that future development reflects the input of your tribe," the Principal Chief concurred. "Cousin, what do you say?"

She nodded her head slowly, thoughtfully. "If we could have this in writing, that would be my choice," she said. "We and our fellow townspeople live in harmony; we do not want to create a rift between us."

"On the other hand," ventured Enoli in his quiet way, "we would prefer not being taken advantage of again."

Everybody nodded in agreement.

When the meeting adjourned several hours later, these decisions had been made:

- To have a legal survey made of the area negotiated by Frederick B. Worthington;

- To notify the City of Dublin of the Eastern Band's inquiry into this issue;

- To require a small, yearly lease from homes, farms, and businesses located within the surveyed area to maintain an indefinite trust fund for the benefit of members of the Cherokee people;

- To develop, in the City of Dublin, a museum to educate visitors about the history of the Cherokee people in the area and their many contributions therein; and

- To incorporate Cherokee history into the public school system of Dublin, Tennessee.

- The documents would be written up by an estate planning lawyer, reviewed by a contract lawyer, and signed when completed by the Principal Chief and appropriate members of the Cherokee Nation and Dublin constituency.

Awinita Morningsong gave her approval to the decisions made. Standing, she said, "My cousin Principal Chief and his Tribal Council members have helped us determine a fair and just end to an old injustice. I am happy there is to be a trust for the benefit of our people, and equally glad to educate the public about our history and the contributions we have made in Eastern Tennessee. Thanks to you all for your wisdom, guidance, and valuable time. May we all prosper in peace and harmony with all." Then she sat and covered her mouth as she yawned.

"This process has tired Grandmother out, but she was determined to come," said Tallulah.

"Truth-Teller told me to come," she said quietly. "I could not refuse."

The attendees looked at her, but there was no further explanation.

The Principal Chief said, "We can adjourn. My cousin isn't the only one who is tired; my wife and I are babysitting our granddaughter while her parents are out of town, and she kept us up a good part of last night."

There were chuckles all around the table, and everyone stood to say goodbye. Representatives of the Eastern Band promised their lawyers would get to work on the legalities as soon as possible.

Before the Dublin contingency left, Enoli asked the Principal Chief, "May I ask a question?"

"Of course. How can I help you?"

"You are the Principal Chief of the Eastern Band of Cherokee Indians, a sovereign nation. Is that equivalent to the President of the United States?"

"I've been asked this question many times, cousin. Our Eastern Band was once part of a much larger Cherokee Nation population, as you undoubtedly know. But after the Cherokee were forcibly removed to Oklahoma, the Nation divided into The Cherokee Nation and United Kituwah Band, in Oklahoma, and the Eastern Band of Cherokee here in North Carolina - both independent nations within a nation.

"So, the answer to your question is yes and no. Yes, in that I am the final word on issues affecting the Eastern Band. But the Principal Chief of the Cherokee in Tahlequah, Oklahoma, governs over four hundred thousand members, many more than we have. In 1924, President Calvin Coolidge signed a bill granting Native Americans full citizenship; consequently, we have dual citizenships. Is that a good answer?"

"Clear as mud," Enole answered with the glimmer of a smile. Then he laughed and shook the Principal Chief's hand again. When they departed, he said to Barney, "I knew all that, but I just wanted to hear it from him. When I joined the Army, I spent four years in Cambodia as a medic, then came home and became a Cherokee healer. I'm proud to be a member of two tribes."

Barney just shook his head and laughed. He really had to get to know his stepfather better.

Once the Dubliners left the building and headed towards their vehicles to return to the motel, Tallulah said to her grandmother "You said you spoke to Truth-Teller Morningsong. How did that happen?"

"I didn't see him, but I heard him clearly," was the answer.

"What did he say?"

"He said it was important for our family to take the papers to the Eastern Cherokee Nation so all people would know the truth of the matter. He said only good would come from this, and it has. He also said I personally should go on his behalf. So, I have done what my grandfather requested."

"And you visited with the Principal Chief again," said Barney.

Awinita smiled. "Yes, that was a very nice bonus," she said with a smile. "My goodness, when I looked at him, I saw my mother in his face. I think of her often."

Barney cleared his throat; he remembered his grandmother with fondness. "As long as we're here, would you like to drive around a little and sightsee?"

His mother smiled. "Yes, that would be nice. It's been a long time since I've been here, and the area is so beautiful. And Barney, as long as we planned to stay the night, may we have dinner where we had lunch? I would love to try the bean bread and squash soup."

"Me, too," Enoli said.

"Sure," Barney laughed as he opened the car doors for his elders. Personally, he planned to stuff himself on the wild meat platter - deer steak, fried fish, and wild hog chops, with a side of cornbread. Oh, yeah!

The Great Somewhere never disappoints, does it? Ever since those old documents were found at the B&B, I've been thinking about how to obtain some retribution for Dublin's Cherokee families. It took a year or so (your time), but I finally met up with Truth-Teller Morningsong. He was surprisingly hard to find as he was preparing for a re-entry. Not all of us do that; many are happy to stay where we are, but some souls wish to experience an earthly experience again for various reasons. Anyhow, we talked for a while about the old documents. Then he told me about his life of being a Native American in the 1800s. I was fascinated and asked if I could help his family out.

In a nutshell, I talked to Barney in a dream to get him motivated, and he took the visit from there. Truth-Teller told me what to say to old Mrs. Morningsong to make sure she would attend the meeting. I'm sorry I left her with the impression she was speaking with her grandfather, but it wasn't much of a stretch of the truth; I passed on his words.

All-in-all I have a good feeling about the outcome. It is just, but kind, and will protect the Cherokee from a further attempted land grab in the future.

It's time (which is just a turn of the phrase here) to go. Janet and I are going to the Friday night high school football game where we'll be cheering on the Dublin Locos. Clickety-clack down the track. Push 'em, push 'em, waaay back! Ah-ooo!

-17-

Matthew and Tallulah

Matthew Boyd, proprietor of M. Boyd Books, was putting a few new volumes on his shelves, trying to ignore the laughter coming from his back room where several groups met on a regular basis. Today it was The Bookenders, a gaggle of mostly women with the occasional gander thrown in. He enjoyed having these groups in his store as they always bought snacks, coffee, tea, and books - lots of books. This month's book choice was apparently an upbeat one as the laughter continued to rise and fall.

The group's leader was Pamela Dodge, a bubbly blonde with an infectious laugh. Today was her birthday and the group had presented her with a t-shirt which proclaimed "Bookmarks Are For Quitters". She'd put it on and trotted out front to show it off to Matthew, who laughed and proclaimed it the perfect gift.

I wish I had the time to join a book club, Matthew thought to himself afterwards. *They have so much fun, and it's not like I'm not surrounded by good reading material.*

It had been a busy year-and-a-half for him. In that short time, he had been shot and nearly killed by an old acquaintance, then regrouped with the help of friends and patrons. He remodeled and expanded his little building to accommodate a tea corner where people could chat and purchase tea and goodies from Mom's Bakery. He had hired a part-time assistant to help with the tea corner and stocking shelves when Matthew wasn't available. Life had gone from friendless to friend-full for this man who had fallen in with a bad crowd at a young age, and spent twenty years in jail for committing a felony.

As Matthew woolgathered about how lucky he was, the cowbell jingled on the front door, and he smiled when he turned to see who had entered. It was Tallulah Morningsong, a first-grade teacher at Dublin Elementary School. They had met in this very place when she came to pick up an order of books for her class at the beginning of the school year. They'd gotten to talking and soon became a couple. Matthew wondered if the time was right to propose. They were alike in so many ways and always had a good time no matter if they were simply cooking a meal, discussing their work, or watching TV. He loved her very much. If he didn't act fast, she might get tired of waiting!

Tallulah entered with a smile on her face, as usual. She wore a butter yellow dress with matching sandals, and her long, black hair was braided, hanging over one shoulder. She literally lit up the room as well as his heart.

I'll do it soon, he promised himself.

"Hello, Matthew", she said warmly. "I missed you this weekend when the family went to Cherokee, but I wouldn't have passed up that opportunity for anything. We accomplished so much. I'll have to tell you all about it soon. What's all the laughing in your back room?"

"The Bookenders are here today."

"Oh, yes, you told me about them. I wish I could attend, but they meet during school hours. Speaking of which, do you have time to fill an order for the school? A very generous donor provided us with enough funds to add books and computers to our library. I have a list of recommended books."

"That's wonderful," Matthew answered. "Yes, I'm free. Let's go to the computer to place the order."

When they sat at his desk next to each other, Tallulah took the list out of her purse. Matthew could smell her favorite perfume, and leaned in a little to appreciate the woody, aromatic fragrance.

"Matthew?" she asked.

"Oh, yes, I was admiring your perfume. Is it English Lavender?"

"Yes, how did you know that?"

"It fell out of your purse one day," he answered. "I picked it up and put it back, but remembered the label." He paused. "It suits you," he whispered, putting his hand over hers. "Tallulah, I've been thinking about us ...".

At that moment, the book club burst out of the meeting room, still in high spirits. "Goodbye, Matthew!" Pamela called and waved. "See you next month!"

He waved back. "Thank you, ladies. I have you on the calendar."

Within twenty seconds the bookstore was quiet again. Tallulah looked at Matthew.

"You were saying?" she asked.

"I was saying that I've been thinking about us, as a couple. I mean, I think we're good together, good for each other, and um, although I don't know how you feel about me, I love you." He breathed out. "There, I've said it. I've been wanting to do it for a long time."

"Shh, don't talk," she said, and kissed him

"Marry me," he said when they came up for air.

"Whenever you like," she whispered in response. "It's almost summer and I won't be working for a couple of months. Pick a date."

As he gathered her in his arms, he whispered in her ear, "I hear June is good for weddings. How about the first day of summer, the twentieth? I think that's a Saturday this year."

"Perfect," she answered with a smile. "I can't wait to tell Grandmother. She's been hoping you would ask me soon."

"Has she, now?" He stood, went to the door, and flipped the sign to CLOSED. They had a lot to talk about, and it wasn't about library books.

-18-

Trey Monroe

In the short time it had been open to the public, Fisher Lake Family Park and Campground had become a huge success due to meticulous planning by owners Barbara Scanlan and her husband Jason Ford. Developing the campground had brought them together, culminating in mutual admiration, and eventually love. Barbara's imagination and love of life had captivated Jason when they first met; and to say she was a beauty was an understatement. In Barbara's eyes, Jason was handsome, far-seeing, savvy in the world of land development and real estate, and had a kind heart. Together they were a handsome and successful pair.

The campground was drawing in long-term visitors as well as day-trippers; there were few businesses in the city that didn't benefit from it financially. Before they left, many of the visitors made reservations for future vacations and weekends.

The working staff were always busy. After the initial start-up period, the campground hummed like a top. Any issues were addressed immediately, but they were infrequent and generally minor. Online reviews remained positive.

Of course, this provided ample opportunities for people looking for work, and the human resources department was kept busy staffing it with competent employees. Among the many applicants was Trey Monroe, former construction worker and equipment operator, unemployed for the past six months due to an accident sustained at home. He told the interviewer he had stepped in a gopher hole and broke his ankle, which was true enough; but he failed to add he had been drunk at the time and could have missed the hole had he been paying attention to where he was walking. Not having been covered by workers compensation, his family was in a desperate situation.

The interviewer listened to his story and obtained a note from the emergency room physician who had treated him, saying his ankle was probably healed sufficiently to return to work. So Trey Monroe was hired as part of the construction and maintenance crew. He couldn't wait to tell Amanda the good news; good wages, insurance, everything he wanted for his family. This would be his big opportunity - and he knew he couldn't afford to mess it up again. The ghost had told him so.

Trey walked into his house with a swagger in his step and a smile on his face.

"Oh, Trey, that's wonderful!" Amanda Monroe exclaimed, beaming at her husband as he related his good news. "When do you begin?"

"They've scheduled me for an eye examination, physical, and drug test in two days," he answered. "I start working Monday." He ran his hand through his thick, blonde hair. "Maybe I should get a haircut, too," he observed. "It's gotten pretty long."

Amanda nodded. "That's a good idea, honey. I have some money set aside; you can have some of that."

Trey cocked his head and squinted one eye. "How'd you save up money?" he asked.

Instinctively, Amanda ducked her head and looked at the floor. "I've been watching Mrs. O'Cain's two little ones for about a month. She's been sick this last trimester, on bedrest. I'm sorry I didn't tell you."

Trey said nothing. He knew why she hadn't told him. Then his face softened into a smile as he chuckled, "Well, we have so many kids, I didn't notice two that weren't our own."

With relief, Amanda smiled back. This was the man she had fallen in love with before alcohol became a problem in their lives. Kissing him lightly on the cheek, she returned to the kitchen where a toddler played with colorful plastic bowls on the floor. "What a pretty hat," she said to the child. "And what color is that?"

"Yeddow!" the child said loudly, removing the bowl from her head and taking up another. "Dis one gween!"

"That's right, Jennifer, you're very smart," she said with proud tears in her eyes. Her children were precious to her; maybe Trey's new job would keep them well-fed, with decent clothes and shoes to avoid being laughed at in school as she had been. Poor little Mandy in her hand-me-downs. The memories were painful, but Amanda vowed she would do whatever she could to give her children the education they deserved, no matter what stood in her way.

Having dropped by the Monroe home, the ghost of Dean Brennan watched Trey proudly relate his happy news.

It's great he found a job, that's step one. And he's currently in very good spirits. But, to an alcoholic, "good spirits" are not always what they're cracked up to be. He needs to keep this job.

"You look very handsome," Amanda gushed upon seeing her husband with his new haircut, clean-shaven face, and wearing a light khaki *Fisher Lake Family Park and Campground* polo shirt with darker trousers. Several of their young children giggled, and three-year-old Susie held her arms out to him. He took up the toddler and hugged her to his chest, then spun her around in a circle while she laughed and shrieked.

"Be careful, Trey," Amanda cautioned, "she just ate breakfast."

"Daddy, can I come with you?" a small boy asked.

"I'm sorry, Andy, you can't go to work with Daddy, but I promise we'll all go to the campground on my day off," Trey answered. The children all hollered with joy, even though a couple didn't know what a campground was.

"We'll have to rent a bus," Amanda said, smiling. "Come have breakfast; you'll be working hard today. And I packed a lunch for you, too."

"Not in the Thomas the Train lunchbox, I hope," Trey said.

"No, that's Andy's. He'd be heartbroken without it. You'll have a paper sack. We'll get you a grown-up lunchbox soon," Amanda promised. "Come have egg biscuits and grits with Ellie, Henry and Reggie, then you better go."

"Yes, ma'am," Trey said, putting Susie back on the ground.

She laughed. "Did I just talk to you like you were six years old? I'm sorry! I so rarely get to talk with adults. I didn't mean it that way, you know, honey."

"I'm not offended. I can imagine how hard it's been for you," he whispered, and kissed his wife on the cheek. "I'm going to mend my ways and be a better man, husband, and father beginning today and forever after."

Trey spent his first day with Maintenance Supervisor, Clay Baker. Clay's grandmother and Awinita Morningsong were sisters, and he had grown up in the Dublin area. His birth name was Red Clay as his maternal grandmother and mother were potters in the old Cherokee tradition. He dropped "Red" from his name when he and his wife moved to Georgia after he was hired as a construction foreman for an industrial development company. But after some time, they returned to Dublin to be with family as they had missed so many birthdays, anniversaries, and family events. Clay was sturdy, tall, and owner of a startlingly large and waxed mustache. Barbara Scanlan liked how the man exuded confidence and commanded respect, and hired him personally as Building Supervisor, which included maintaining and modifying the structures on site.

Trey followed Clay around the first day, learning where everything was, what new construction was underway, where repairs or upgrades were needed, where the equipment sheds were, and the protocol for assigning tools and machinery. Trey was familiar with many of the carpentry tools; he had also operated forklifts, backhoes and off-road trucks in his prior job.

As they rode around the area in his off-road truck, Clay peppered Trey with questions to assess his new employee's skills, knowledge, and personality.

"So, where are you from?" he asked, as they headed towards the trailhead to the national forest. "Born in Dublin?"

"Yessir, I was. Went to school here, married my high school sweetheart, and have six or seven children now," Trey answered.

"Six or seven?"

Trey laughed. "Seven, but two are identical twins; can't tell those boys apart without looking at their teeth. Henry lost a canine tooth that may never grow back. If it doesn't, Amanda - that's my wife - says we should have the dentist make him a gold one so we can tell the boys apart. They're in sixth grade."

"Haha, I like your wife already," Clay laughed, and stopped his truck by the trailhead. "Well, here is the new project. We've just gotten approval from Great Smoky Mountains National Park to open two trails here, one long, one short. I've got the specs here," he said, reaching for paperwork on his dashboard. "The short trail will run in a circle from this parking lot for a mile and a half and will be wheelchair accessible, or for those who don't want to walk too far. It intersects with the longer train twice, as you see here, but will be clearly marked as the short trail so nobody makes a wrong turn and winds up on the four-mile trail. And even if that happens, there will be multi-language signs advising wheelchairs to turn around to return to the campground. Those on the long trail can catch the short trail to return if they can't make it all the way around."

"Sounds like safety first," Trey said. "I don't think you've missed a thing."

"Yes, absolutely. And to top it off, if someone is on one of the trails after it closes at sunset, there are motion-activated cameras all along both so we can find them. We've visited many trails and read current literature on safe hiking, so while some experienced hikers might consider it tame in some respects, even on the short trail they'll experience plenty of forest, brooks, and flora and fauna to keep it interesting."

"I'm impressed," Trey said.

Clay turned to Trey and said, "Monroe, I want to put you on this project. We need equipment operators to clear the trails, build bridges over the brooks, and so on. We'll have a cement company lay the short trail, and are getting bids for the electronics required, signs, and botanists to identify any dangerous plants. We start work on this next week, and in the meantime, you'll shadow a couple of other guys in Maintenance to get the feel of the place; our team has a hand in everything."

Trey could barely contain his enthusiasm. This was perfect, right up his alley, respectful work. His family will be proud of him. Then he asked, "How long do you think this project will take?"

"I was just getting to that," Clay answered. "We think two months for the entire trail system. I think we can get the short trail done in four weeks since we've already got contracts for the work, equipment, materials and specialists."

Four weeks! Trey was astonished, but Clay smiled behind his mustache. "It's all in the planning, Monroe. We have a good team and a good plan. Let's get back to the Maintenance office and I'll show you the maps and time schedule." Then he paused and said, "I'm glad you got hired on, Monroe. You have the experience with equipment, and I suspect the talent to help us get this project in on time."

"Thank you, sir," Trey said after a few seconds. "I'll do my very best for you." And he meant it.

-19-

Amanda's New Job

Amanda Monroe had put her feet up for five minutes before the phone rang. She was used to living with intermittent sleep and rest, but after seven children in twice that many years, she felt more tired lately. She knew she wasn't expecting, but she felt age catching up with her. Tending to her family was a full-time job; if she wasn't cooking, washing and drying clothes, cleaning the house, or supervising the older children's homework, she caught an hour or two of rest before the babies woke up for their nighttime feedings. And it was hard to keep track of everyone's needs, which now included Trey's uniform maintenance. She rarely had time to stop and chat with anyone her own age. Thirty-three wasn't old, but she longed to converse with adults once in a while.

So when the phone rang, she secretly hoped it was someone she might chat with for a few minutes before the older kids came home from school, and the youngest awoke from their afternoon naps.

"Hello?" she answered.

"Hello, is this Amanda Monroe?" the woman asked.

"Yes, I'm Amanda."

"Mrs. Monroe, my name is Ruth Sutton. I'm the assistant to the Human Resources Director at Fisher Lake Recreational Campground. Do you have a few minutes?"

"Yes. Is my husband all right?" she asked immediately fearing the worst.

"Oh, yes, Mr. Monroe is fine. In fact, he asked me to call you."

Amanda was puzzled. "He did?"

Ms. Sutton chuckled. "Yes, let me tell you what this call is about. We have on our campus a very good child care center, as you might have heard. Our staff watches children for various reasons, mostly when adults would prefer they stay somewhere safe when the parents are canoeing, sailing, hiking - that sort of thing. Sometimes the children are there for a few hours, some longer, depending on their parents' plans. With me so far?"

"Yes."

"Well, between the fact that the campground is experiencing more visitors than ever now that the weather is warm, and one of our children's caregivers is moving away, we find ourselves looking for an experienced person to help us out. Your husband happened to see the help wanted sign in the office this morning, and suggested we call you to see if you were interested in the position."

"Me?" Amanda laughed. "I have seven children and a husband to care for. There aren't enough hours in the day to just do that."

"Before you say no, Mrs. Monroe, let me give you some information," Ms. Sutton said quickly. "First, it's a part-time position under the supervision of our licensed Child Care Director. Second, it pays very well. Third, there are company benefits we could discuss, if you are interested. Fourth, the hours are from nine a.m. to one p.m., four hours a day, Monday through Friday. We have two other part-time people working overlapping shifts, from seven a.m. to seven p.m. when the center closes."

Amanda's mind was whirling. "Wouldn't I have to be certified to be a childcare worker?" she asked.

"The Child Care Center is licensed, and the Director is certified, but you wouldn't have to be. Of course, all of our employees must have a thorough background check before hire, which meets the requirement for this position. Our center is virtually monitored, meaning there are cameras in all rooms which are watched in real-time by our security company. Still with me?"

"Yes, yes I am," Amanda answered. "But who would watch my little ones while I'm at work?"

"I hadn't gotten around to that yet", Ruth Sutton said, sensing Amanda's interest. "Your children who are not yet in school would attend free of charge, excluding bottles, formula, diapers and so forth which you would have to provide."

"Bottles, diapers, juice boxes, snacks." Amanda muttered. "Ms. Sutton, may I have a day to discuss this with my husband? I'm very interested, but I need to run this past him before accepting a position outside the home."

"Absolutely, Mrs. Monroe. I'm here from nine to five tomorrow. From what Mr. Monroe said this morning, you're a perfect fit for this job, immensely qualified, and a good and kind person."

"Thank you so much," Amanda whispered, as if she had just received the highest praise in her life. Trey valued her as a person - that meant the world to her. "I'll give you a call tomorrow, I promise," she said before their goodbyes. She couldn't wait to talk with Trey this evening!

All of the Monroes enjoyed spaghetti with meatballs. The big kids slurped and made funny faces when the noodles rebounded on their faces. The little ones played with it on their high chairs and smeared it on their faces, ingesting a little of it by accident, supplementing their baby food. The twins had meatball races on the table until Trey saw them and put a stop to it. So although spaghetti night was always fun, it was also always messy. The littlest three - Jennifer, Susie, and Andy, never wore shirts on spaghetti night, and were bathed immediately afterwards. And there was much clean-up required at the dinner table, too. So by the time everyone had been bathed, showered, and the kitchen cleaned, it was eight o'clock.

Although Trey helped with the children, it was obvious he was tired after a long day of outdoors work. But he was in good spirits at the end of this first week, and Amanda was feeling secure for the first time in their married lives. Still, she hesitated bringing up the subject of her job offer at the child care center.

"Trey," she said, as she put the spaghetti pot away, "Ruth Sutton from the campground 's H.R. Department called me today."

"Zat so?" he said, sitting at the now-clean kitchen table. "What did you talk about?"

"Oh, Trey, she told me you recommended me for the open position at the child care center. We talked for quite a while and she told me all about it, the pay, the benefits, and so on. By the time the call was over I'd made up my mind. I would love to work there. With my extra money, we could even put a little aside for emergencies. One of the benefits was free child care for the little ones. The twins, Ellie, and Teddy can walk over to the Morning Glory B&B after school. I called Mrs. O'Mooney and she told me it would be fine; the children can do their homework in the dining room, as they'd be there between meals, and could walk home together after I get home. It's a wonderful opportunity, and I'd still have time to keep up the house and cook meals. Are you all right with these arrangements?"

"How would you get there and back?" Trey asked. "We don't live that close to the campground, and you'd have three little children to tote around."

"I mentioned that to Ms. Sutton, too," Amanda answered. "Believe it or not, she has an old VW Beetle she's willing to loan us until we can get a second car for me. Babies don't need leg room, so two car seats would fit in the back, and Andy could sit up front with me."

Trey chuckled. "You've got it all planned out already, don't you? Well, I think we could work with this. I wondered about transportation, but Ms. Sutton came through for us. She's a very nice lady, kind of a grandma type. She told me she'd been ready to retire after more than thirty years in the human resources business; but she took this job at *Fisher Lake* since Hank Scanlan had been her uncle. This was his farm where she spent a lot of time when she was a youngster."

"I love how everybody knows everybody in Dublin," Amanda said. "So I take it this is good for you, honey? I'll call her tomorrow morning and let her know I'll take the position."

Trey stood up and put his arms around his wife. "You know, Amanda, if this job becomes too much for you, there's no shame in quitting."

"Yes, but I'd also be with adults, and I've been wanting to help out financially for a long time. Three hundred dollars a week would be a big help, even if just to save for emergencies. I'm very excited about this, Trey. For the first time in my life, I'll be paid for doing what I already know."

"Nobody knows children like you do, Amanda," he agreed. "Oh, look," he said, pulling back from their embrace. "I see a little spaghetti sauce on your lip. Let me get that off."

"Oh, Trey!" she giggled before he kissed her again.

-20-

A Lot Going On at the Mullen's

"Hi, Stacey, I'm home!" Dr. Joe Mullen called as he entered his house, deftly avoiding a large composition of colorful building blocks piled close to the front door.

"In the kitchen!" his wife called out. "Watch your step! Paisley has been building houses again."

"I see that. Where's my little princess?" he called.

"Dada, Dada!" an almost-toddler screamed with delight from the kitchen, wheeling into the living room on her baby jumperoo, her little feet pushing fast against the floor.

"There you are," Joe smiled, scooping his squirming daughter up in his arms and kissing her fat cheeks. "Have you been playing construction boss again, Paisley? I see your new houses and a few carpenters."

Stacey walked into the living room, wiping her hands on a dish towel. "Actually," she said, "this is a new hotel. The monkey is tiling around the pool, the giraffe is painting the high parts, the zebra is painting the low parts, and the elephant is in charge of landscaping."

"Aha, I see," Joe replied. "Paisley has been busy, but how was your day, Stace?"

"You're a riot," she answered. "How was yours?"

Joe shifted the baby to his other arm and leaned in to kiss his wife. "Actually, we were pretty busy. We had two new patients, and I had a meeting with Julian about accommodating another AA group."

They moved into the kitchen where Stacey added chopped tomato to a tossed salad.

"Dada, Dada, Dada," Paisley sang in Joe's arms. He kissed her again, then put her on the floor next to a kitchen chair. The baby pulled herself up and stood there wobbling back and forth for a few seconds, then plopped down onto her diapered bottom, laughing.

"Looks like she'll be toddling pretty soon," he beamed. "How about that?"

"I can't wait," Stacey deadpanned. "She's fast as a bullet with that jumperoo, but at least I can hear it and know where she is. She can't fall out of it, either. I wish I could really grow eyes in the back of my head."

"I understand," Joe nodded. "Our lives will never be the same again with this little tornado around."

Stacey turned to look at Joe with a sigh. "You're right, but Joe, have a seat. I have something to tell you."

"What, honey, are you all right? Is Paisley okay?"

"Yes, of course, we're both fine. But I hope you are after I tell you that ... we're going to have another baby."

Joe stared at her, then sat down. Paisley pulled herself up by holding onto his pants and stood there swaying and smiling at her accomplishment. "Another baby? Are you sure?" he asked.

"Well, that's what the home pregnancy tests indicated; I did two of them to make sure. And I know the signs of pregnancy now. I called Mercy Hogan's office to make an appointment in two days, but I'm sure she'll confirm my suspicions. Joe? You're so quiet, what are you thinking?"

To answer her question, Joe scooped Paisley up again, spun her around and hollered, "Whoopee!" as the baby laughed. She was going to be a big sister!

"So how are the AA groups going?" Stacey asked as she poured her husband a cup of coffee - the coffee she sniffed and longed for, but couldn't have according to her doctor.

Joe thought for a moment while he pressed the lever on the toaster. "I think they're going very well," he answered. "I'm glad they're addressing their addiction to alcohol." He looked around the room. "Where's Paisley?"

"She fell asleep in her playpen so I left her there. I'm always afraid I'll trip over her, especially in the kitchen."

Joe removed the toast, and brought it to the table. "Do you want one, Stace?" he asked. "I made two in case you felt like eating this morning."

"I am hungry," she admitted. "I'll have toast with chamomile tea to warm up the baby."

"When is your ultrasound again?" Joe asked.

"Friday at three," she answered. "Will you be there, honey, since we might decide to know the baby's sex?"

"Yes, and I want to hear its heartbeat like we did with Paisley," Joe said, smiling. "I'll ask Paloma to clear my calendar for that time. I usually don't have many appointments on Friday afternoon."

"I like Paloma," Stacey said as she poured boiling water into a cup. "Is she still planning to attend medical school? Julian would love that."

"As far as I know she hasn't changed her mind. Julian says she's considering gerontology so she can take care of him and

Elena in their old age. I think he was joking, but whatever she chooses she'd be good at it. I'll be sad to see her go, though."

"Gerontology is a much-needed specialty", Stacey mused. "She'd be sought out, that's for sure." Returning to the table with her hot water and a teabag, she said, "Getting back to your new group, it continues to surprise me that there is such a need for Alcoholics Anonymous in this area. Dublin has taverns and restaurants that serve beer and liquor, and a couple of liquor stores, too. The constant temptation of these places must be difficult for alcoholics."

"That's part of the equation. Genetics, upbringing, and stress are factors, too. People sometimes drink to relax, which is fine unless it gets out of control. You can't really put a finger on any one cause."

"So I guess your members have different backgrounds but the same problems. That must make it hard for people to relate with each other," Stacey said.

"Sometimes, but that's generally because there are other issues they're working through as well. That's when we offer individual counseling. It's more focused work, more time with me providing direct feedback," Joe answered.

They'd had this conversation a few times over the years, so he wondered why Stacey was bringing it up again. "Is something bothering you, Stace?"

She took a sip of tea before answering. "You know about my parents' problems with alcohol," she said. "Now that we're going to have another baby, I started wondering if those genes have been passed down to our children."

"You've never had the temptation to drink, have you?" Joe asked.

Stacey shook her head. "You know me, honey. I was always too busy with school and being at church all the time; I never had even a glass of champagne until the day I graduated college. Alcohol doesn't appeal to me at all, but if there's a genetic component, it does concern me." Polishing off her toast, she added, "Is there a lab test to see if alcoholism is genetically predisposed?"

Joe stood up. "I need more toast, how about you?" he asked, opening the bread bag. Stacey nodded. "To answer your question, yes, there are easy cheek swab DNA tests people can take to identify the so-called "addiction genes", but it's not an exact science for determining predisposition. Results are generally forty to sixty percent positive. If you have a gene for a particular condition or trait, it only means you have a higher-than-average chance of developing it."

"I guess that answers my question," she finally said after finishing off her tea. She paused for a moment, then said, "Oh, Joe, put your hand right here." She put his hand over her stomach and watched his face as the baby kicked several times.

"Wow, possibly a soccer player," he smiled. "Does it happen a lot?"

"Only when I need a nap," she answered.

"Poor baby," Joe said, wrapping his arms around her. "How do women do this?"

Stacey smiled. "Someone has to."

Stacey's ultrasound appointment was scheduled for Friday at 8:30 a.m. It was a hectic morning, especially since Paisley was a little cranky with a tooth coming in, but they did manage to get to Dr. Hogan's office on time. Joe was as restless as his daughter; Stacey was the calmest of the three.

At 8:28, a technician called them into the ultrasound room. Awed by the strange room, Paisley became quiet. Joe held her in his arms as the technician prepped Stacey and began the test.

Twenty minutes later, they met with Mercy Hogan in her office to review the results.

"It's nice to see you all again. You've grown a lot in the last few months, haven't you, Paisley?"

By way of an answer, Paisley stuck her thumb in her mouth.

Stacey and Joe looked at each other anxiously, and Dr. Hogan didn't miss their body language.

Smiling at them, she said, "The results of your ultrasound shows you have a healthy little—do you want to know if you're having a boy or girl?"

"Yes!" Joe and Stacey answered at the same time. "I can't stand the suspense," Joe said.

"Then here's your answer - it's a boy. Congratulations!"

Back at home, Joe bounced around like he had springs on his shoes. His wife and daughter watched him with much amusement.

"I hope you have this much energy when the baby arrives," Stacey said. "There's no backing out now."

"I'm as happy as a man could be," Joe said, kissing her on the forehead. "I love you both, and I'll love the new one, too. Now we have to decide what his name will be."

Paisley pulled her thumb out of her mouth and said, "Wobin".

Joe and Stacey stared at each other, then Stacey said, "I think she means Robin. We watched Sesame Street this morning and she loves that character. This is amazing! Her first real word after Dada and Mama is Robin."

"Then Robin it is," Joe said, glad his daughter's favorite muppet wasn't Fozzie or Gonzo. Then he waltzed her around the living room singing "When the red, red robin comes bob, bob bobbin' along..."

Stacey took a video for when she needed a laugh. Motherhood's not for sissies.

-21-

Out to Lunch

The Chew-Chew Diner was a landmark in Dublin. Owned by Bobby and Dottie Green, it was a popular gathering space for anyone craving a hearty Southern breakfast, or a tasty meat-and-two lunch with a glass of sweet tea. Dottie had requested her cook to branch out a few years ago and add a signature Chew-Chew Burger, a chicken salad sandwich, two vegetarian dishes, and a few appetizers including fried green tomatoes. She had heard that tourists sometimes had no way to keep leftovers cold, so she and Bobby added smaller-sized meals to accommodate tourists and children. Pastries from Mom's Bakery were always available, as were Dottie's much-requested chocolate and lemon icebox pies. Consequently, the Chew-Chew was packed from six in the morning until six in the evening.

Sometimes people didn't come specifically for the food, but to watch the antique Lionel train set that ran through both dining rooms, making a ten-minute circuit of the diner. It smoked and clacked over their heads, and occasionally tooted its whistle. That project had been Bobby's, and over the years he'd put a lot of effort and love into it, not only adding various cars to the steam engine, but producing a soundtrack that played through the sound system. He even painted tiny murals on the walls to enhance the experience. Children of all ages came to see - and eat - while they were in Dublin.

One mid-week afternoon, a weary Stacey Mullen entered the diner, holding her daughter's little hand. Paisley had begun to toddle, so Stacey decided to earmark the event. They walked slowly through the door, but when Paisley saw all the people inside, she hesitated. Dottie saw them and hurried over.

"Oh, my, Pastor, what a nice surprise! Is this your little Paisley? She's quite the beauty!" Dottie cooed, smiling at the toddler as Stacey picked her up.

"Yes she is to both questions," answered Stacey. "Gosh, you calling me Pastor made me wonder who you were talking to for a moment. It feels like forever since I've given a sermon at Open Arms Church. How are you, Mrs. Green?"

"Busy, busy, and we wouldn't have it any other way," was the answer. "Please come visit with Bobby for a second while we clear a table for you."

In a few minutes, the mother and daughter were seated at a table for two, one of the chairs having been replaced with a highchair. Katie, their server, took Stacey's order for a bowl of Dottie's macaroni and cheese to share with Paisley, a slice of lemon icebox pie, and a glass of ice water. Paisley's sippy cup was filled part-way with water, too. Stacey longed for a big glass of tea or a cup of coffee but Dr. Hogan had advised her to forgo caffeine. No wonder she was so tired all the time; she needed perking up and those huge prenatal vitamins weren't doing the trick.

Lunch came, and thankfully Paisley decided she liked macaroni and cheese. Stacey put two spoonsful on a little plate for her because Paisley was learning how to feed herself with her hands. Relieved, Stacey picked up her fork, but as she took a bite of her meal, the toddler grabbed a little fistful and flung mac and cheese across the table, some of it landing on Stacey's white blouse. Jumping up from her chair in order to disarm

Paisley's other fist, Stacey knocked over her glass of icy cold water which splashed over her linen pants, causing her to gasp.

Dottie and Katie rushed to the table with cloths and napkins, while Stacey looked down at her potentially ruined blouse and soaked pants. As Dottie patted them with a clean towel, and Katie cleaned Paisley off, Stacey broke into tears.

"I'm a terrible mother!" she cried. "I can't even do something simple like take my child out to eat. What was I thinking? My blouse is ruined and everybody is looking at me!"

Dottie took the sobbing woman by the shoulders and gathered her into her arms. "You're not a terrible mother, you're a normal mother." Turning, she said quietly to Katie, "Would you take charge of Paisley for a few minutes while I see if I can get this stain out of her blouse before it sets?" Katie nodded. Then to Stacey, she said, "Katie has four little nieces and nephews so Paisley's in good hands."

In the ladies' restroom, Dottie carefully removed a bit of macaroni from Stacey's blouse, then wet the cloth with cold water. Using hand soap, she gently rubbed in a circular motion. "There," she said, smiling. "I think we got it in time. Wash it in cold water when you get home and it should be okay. Here's a paper towel to blot it. You should wash your face, too."

Stacey stood still, tears in her eyes. "Mrs. Green, thank you so much for your help. I find myself going in three directions at once now that my daughter is toddling, and I'm not sleeping very well because she's cutting another tooth. Poor Joe is so tired, he just crashes after dinner."

"And you're expecting again," Dottie smiled gently.

"How did you know? We haven't told anybody."

"Honey, I've had six children, so I know a thing or two. I can see it in your face, the way you move, your hair has changed, lots of other little clues."

"That's amazing," Stacey said as she patted her face with a wet paper towel. "I never knew." Tossing the paper towel in the trash can, she said with a sigh, "I wish my mother was here. Even though we don't exactly see eye to eye, I could use some female commiseration. Joe wants to help, but it's not the same."

"No, it's not the same," Dottie agreed. "But how about this - if you like, I'll be your surrogate mother for as long as you need me, okay?"

"Oh, I couldn't burden you with my problems, Mrs. Green. You're so busy with the diner, I can't impose on you that way."

"Pooh! It wouldn't be an imposition, it would be an honor," Dottie said. "My children are grown up and some don't live nearby anymore. And please call me Dottie. Mrs. Green sounds so formal, and I think we're past formality, don't you? I'll call you Stacey, not Pastor."

And so it happened that whenever Stacey Mullen needed to talk, she knew who to see or call on the phone. And Paisley grew to love her surrogate grandparents, even more than she loved macaroni and cheese and the choo-choo train that made her laugh every time the whistle blew.

-22-

The AA Meeting

A group of ten men occupied the small conference room of the Dublin Healing Center, an office building where the offices of Julian Hernandez, MD, and Joseph Mullen, Psy.D were located. A large oval conference table surrounded by a dozen chairs sat in the middle of the room, and a credenza at one end held carafes of coffee, ice water, disposable cups, and so on.

When the wall clock indicated it was 7:00 p.m., a man stood up to speak. "Hello, everyone, my name is Charlie. Most of you know me, but a few don't. That's okay. Just remember that anything said in this room remains in this room. It is not to be shared with anyone, friends or family. You can feel free to speak what's on your mind without fear of embarrassment or derision by anyone here, okay?"

Nods from everyone.

Charlie continued. "I'm in charge of the meeting tonight, so you new guys just follow along. Let's start with the AA Preamble."

"Okay," he said when the short mission statement ended, "before we discuss today's meditation, does anyone have anything to get off your chest?"

Trey Monroe looked around the table. He was slightly embarrassed to be here, and may not have come had it not been for Amanda's encouragement and the former mayor's ghostly intervention. He knew several of these men; he'd even gone to school with one - did that guy remember him? What had brought them all to this group? He supposed his story wasn't much different than any of theirs; his family used alcohol as a way to forget their problems, and as an excuse for everything that went wrong in their lives. But this commitment to stay sober and never backslide - well, was that even possible? Forever is a long time. And once you're sober, if you DO backslide, you have to start all over with the twelve steps. He felt panic rising in his chest and almost stood to leave, but Charlie was speaking again.

"Nobody? Okay, then let's do our daily meditation."

Trey took a long, deep breath as he took a sheet of paper and passed the rest to the man seated next to him. He looked down; the topic was "Forgive Yourself". Charlie began to read the short, but powerful piece which ended with, "God forgave you long ago. Why don't you forgive yourself?"

Charlie looked around the room after finishing the meditation, his eyes resting a moment on Trey's as he said, "Forgiving and being honest with yourself can be hard to do, especially when you've spent years pretending you don't have a problem with alcohol. But hearing the stories of other people who are experiencing the same disease is helpful. You don't have to lie to anyone here, including yourself. Follow the steps, learn how to handle your problem, and you will be a happier and healthier person. So, any discussion?"

As someone raised his hand to speak, Trey swallowed hard. He couldn't count the number of times he'd berated himself for "messing up" or "not doing something right", then self-medicating with alcohol. He heard Dean's voice in his head telling him he'd hit the bottom and it was up to him to dig his way out. Well, perhaps he was powerless over alcohol, but maybe, just maybe, this was his shovel. Amanda and the children were his highest priority; they depended on him. As he looked around the room at the men in the circle, he understood they were all on the same page. They wanted to live sober lives, too. For the first time in a long while, Trey heard the angel on his shoulder say, "I'm proud of you." Funny, it sounded a little like the old mayor.

I'm impressed with Trey Monroe, Dean thought as he stood behind Trey Monroe, hoping nobody would sense him there. *Janet always saw the good in people, that's just one reason I married her. So did Don Ryan, always doing for others without a thought of compensation for his legal pro bono work. I'll do the same for Monroe but I know the urge to drink is as strong as any physical craving. His wife and children need him clean and sober.*

And with that, Dean poofed himself back to Janet because they had tickets to see the Angelic Orchestra perform Symphony No. 3 (Eroica), conducted by the composer himself, Ludwig von Beethoven. Janet would be upset if they missed one precious note. Next week, though, was Hank Williams and Patsy Cline!

"I don't care if a volcano erupts in downtown Knoxville, Janet, I'm not missing that one!" he had told her.

-23-

Repent!

It was week four at True Faith Church and Jacob Ezel was preparing his music and notes for the Sunday sermon when he heard a commanding voice from on high.

"Jacob, do you know who this is? That's right - it's me! There are a few things you badly need to hear so listen carefully. First, if someone knows the right thing to do but doesn't do it, that's a sin. And conversely, if someone knows what he's doing is wrong but does it anyway, that's also a sin. Second, sin is lawlessness, for which there are always repercussions. And third, 'Anyone who has been stealing must steal no longer, but must work, doing something useful with their own hands, that they may have something to share with those in need.'[2] So figure it out, Jake. You've spent your whole life sinning; it's time to change before it's too late!"

"But, but ... I don't know how to change! What would I do? I have no education, no training, no friends to turn to for help!" Jake exclaimed, staring around him to see his accuser, and hoping no burning bush erupted in front of him.

"I'll say it again, Jake. Figure it out. Return the money, confess before the law takes things into its own hands, talk to a counselor or a real minister, turn your mind to doing good for all instead of concentrating on your own selfish benefit. You're not the first to stray off the path of righteousness, but you can step back on." *(Wow, I was charged up now; wish I'd thought of all this when I was a young man!)*

Jake fell to his knees, body shaking, hands in supplication.

"I'll be watching you, Jacob," the ghost of Dean Brennan said, his voice dramatically fading away. "Stray again and suffer the consequences!"

Slowly getting to his feet, Jake wondered if what he had experienced was real or the product of his vivid imagination. No, in a million years he wouldn't have imagined that - it had happened, it was real. The Almighty had told him he must mend his ways, or else. He didn't want to think about what "the consequences" would be. Jake heard the voice in this church, and its meaning was clear.

An hour after his encounter, Jake surprised his congregants by walking to the piano without saying a word. He sat for ten seconds with his eyes closed, then put his hands on the keyboard. But rather than the psalms or songs he had written, he sang a song he'd learned on the cruise ship. Only this time he performed it slowly, quietly, and with emotion.

"I have sinned, dear Father, Father I have sinned.

Try and help me, Father, won't you let me in?

Sire, I have stolen, stolen many times.

Raised my voice in anger when I know I never should.

Father, please forgive me.

Please, will you direct me the right way?

Liar! That's what they keep calling me.

Liar! Every day, every night."

When he finished the song, Jake stood and walked to the podium. People looked at each other, bewildered. This was not the Reverend Jacob Ezel they knew, the man on a mission. This man was broken and weak.

"Friends, that song, written by the rock group Queen, should be my anthem," Jake said quietly. "All my life I have wanted things that others had - good looks, sophistication, money, fame, you name it. But I was poor and undereducated, so I ignorantly figured the only way to have those things was to steal them. I have spent my life cheating and lying, but I am confessing to you today, as a man who has heard the voice of The Almighty, that today is the beginning of a new way of life for Jacob Ezel. I lied about being a minister, about having a degree, about everything I may have said about myself to impress you and, yes, about Love For Africa. I promise to return your money and will tell Mr. Ford I have to renege on the lease for this building. And I'll leave Dublin as soon as I can find somewhere to go."

Jake paused for a moment; the congregation was silent. "I want to thank you all for your love and support. You're good people and it was wrong of me to take advantage of you. There is too much corruption in the world, and I'm deeply ashamed to have been a part of it. At least I will leave Dublin with my chin up rather than sneaking out in the middle of the night as I've done in the past."

That was it. Jake stepped off the podium and headed towards his office. He heard people leaving, the front doors slamming. Putting his face in his hands, he began to cry.

"Jacob, that was a powerful confession," the voice said.

Jake's head jerked up. He saw nothing, but he knew what he'd heard.

"If you are serious about turning your life around, I will help you. You, like all humans, have free will, but I strongly suggest you pay attention to the signs I will set out for you."

"Yes, Lord, I will!" Jake cried out.

:"Excellent. First, make good on the promises you made to the congregation; return their money and speak with Jason Ford about your lease. The signs will begin tomorrow morning - keep your eyes and ears and, most of all, your heart open." Dean's voice faded away with, "I have faith in you, Jacob."

Jake awoke at dawn on Monday with not a little trepidation in his resolve. Maybe what he'd experienced was the result of too much booze over the years. Who knows, but the damage was already done. His congregation had left him and rumors would already be flying left and right.

Hungry, he looked in his little refrigerator but it was empty. He'd have to go out for breakfast, but the Chew-Chew Diner was closed for a few days as the worn floors were being replaced. There weren't any fast food places in Dublin. Wait, someone at church had mentioned there was a breakfast buffet at the new hotel a few blocks from Jake's apartment, and you could call in and pick up your order even if you weren't a guest. Jake found the number and called it.

An automated message asked him to hold, and he grumbled, as did his stomach. As he waited, he heard the following: "Thank you for holding. We'll be with you as soon as possible. In the meantime, please enjoy a moment of the sound of rain on a tin roof."

What the heck, Jake wondered as the gentle pattering began. It was better than canned music, he had to say. Thirty seconds later, the pleasant voice said, "Thank you for continuing to hold. As a service to our community, we recommend calling the Dublin Chamber of Commerce at 555-0615 to hear a list of open positions with our Chamber business members. That's 555-0615. Thank you for holding. Someone will be with you ..."

"Hotel Dublin, good morning. How may I assist you?"

Jake was more than a little confused, but he managed to order buttermilk pancakes, a side of bacon, and coffee before saying, "While I was on hold I heard the automated message about the Chamber of Commerce job listings. That's a great service to the community."

The young man on the other end of the line said, "Sir, I picked up the phone in two rings. You weren't on hold, I promise. Anyway, your order will be ready in fifteen minutes - thanks for calling." The phone clicked off.

Jake stared at his cell phone for a full minute. What in the world ... and then he remembered his conversation with The Almighty the previous day. It was a sign! Now, what was that number again, he asked himself as he rummaged for a pen and paper. If he couldn't find one, he'd just head over to the Chamber of Commerce after breakfast.

I never saw my wife, Janet, so happy. She was laughing and shimmering with delight.

"I understand how you feel now, Dean," she said to me. "I feel so good helping Jake Ezel out this way. It was a brainstorm on your part."

"Now, Janet, you did all the work. You wrote the script, provided the sound effects, and narrated it perfectly. You get all the credit for this one," I said.

"Do you think he'll call that number?" she asked.

"Yes, he wrote it down correctly. Jake may be a con man, but he actually has a soft spot. He's never physically hurt anybody, just disappointed them. Maybe he'll be able to redeem himself by taking an honest job."

"Oh, I hope so, dear," Janet said. "But let's keep an eye on him."

Those were my thoughts exactly as we whooshed away to check on our family, which had continued to grow with the birth of another grandson.

A few days later, Jacob Ezel had been hired to play piano at The Old Train Station, working most evenings from four to ten p.m. He played everything from ragtime to classical, as well as performing his own compositions. Not only had Jake been forgiven for trying to scam money from his parishioners since he had returned their donations, but he was making more money than he ever dreamed of and enjoying every moment of it.

Joel Turner was pleased to add him to the staff of The Old Train Station since this restaurant and gift shop had been his pet project in the revitalization of Dublin. Jake's musical skills were receiving rave reviews, as were the quality of food and service. Reservations skyrocketed, and Jake's reputation over the ensuing months enabled him to upgrade his living situation from a motel room to a new apartment where he had stability and a place to compose. His crisis had become the answer to a new life - with a little help from Dean.

-24-

Reality Check

Lauren O'Mooney was still in shock when she returned to the Morning Glory B&B after hearing Jacob Ezel's confession. Her head spun with his admission of guilt and his promise to return all their money. She never thought she'd have been taken in by a con man - everything he'd said and demonstrated had seemed true. She'd felt him to be an honest man, full of good intentions and love for all people, not a cunning trickster who just diverted their money into his own pockets. There was no Peter Vandeker, there was no Love For Africa. She had wanted to be helpful and kind, but only felt used and foolish.

Heading for her room, she was stopped by Hayden at the bottom of the stairs as he walked towards her with a framed canvas in his hands.

"I didn't expect you back so soon, Lauren. I was going to put this in the Rose Suite as a surprise for you." When he saw her face, he stopped. "Is everything all right?"

"No," she answered shakily, "it's not all right. I've been such a fool," she said, wiping a tear from her eye.

"Do you want to tell me what happened?" he asked gently, setting the canvas down, leaning it against the staircase.

"Not here, Hayden, and not right now. I need to pull myself together first. Do you have a little time in about an hour?"

"Sure," he answered. "I'll bring this to your room then. Are you sure you're okay?"

Lauren nodded and smiled. "Yes, thank you for your kindness, Hayden. I'll see you in a little while."

The following morning, Izzy loaded Lauren's bags into her replacement rental car. She had decided not to fly to Indianapolis - it was a short flight and a waste of money. A long car ride would give her time to think and decide what to do next. She was bringing a few of Hayden's watercolors with her, but in her heart of hearts, she knew these were the last she would receive. Not that she wanted more; she didn't want a lot of artwork in the studio if she decided to sell the place. After all, a new owner would want to stock their own works. If Hayden wanted to continue selling his watercolors he could find a local gallery with no problem, considering his reputation.

When she told Hayden and Fiona she was leaving, their reaction wasn't what she had thought it would be. She had assumed they would be glad to see her go, but it was as if they honestly would miss her presence and wished her well. They made it clear she was invited to visit anytime. She had learned a lot about herself these past few years. Since visiting the little city of Dublin, she had become less selfish and money-oriented. She appreciated the serenity of wandering through the morning glories at the B&B. And even after what had happened at True Faith Missionary Church and her ready acceptance of Jake Ezel's so-called ministry, she had become less cynical of people. Hayden, Fiona, the staff of the Morning Glory B&B, even little Ellie, had impressed her with their kindness.

When she left, everyone walked her to her car to bid her goodbye. Driving away with a tear in her eye and a sack lunch from Curly Pete, Lauren felt uplifted and loved for the first time in years. She felt herself blossom inside like a morning glory in full bloom. Maybe today's flower will only last one day, but the vine will produce flowers as long as it lives. Like we do, she thought as she turned off Morning Glory Lane onto Broad Street, heading home.

-25-

The Good, the Bad, and the Best

"Happy anniversary, Stace!" Joe beamed as he entered the kitchen. With a big card in one hand and a box of candy in the other, he bent down and planted a kiss on Stacey's cheek. She was watching Paisley eat organic dry cereal shaped like tiny bunnies, making sure her daughter took a sip of diluted organic apple juice after each bite.

"Oh, thank you, honey," she said, not taking her eyes off Paisley. "I have a card for you, too; I'll get it after Paisley's done in a few minutes."

"No rush," Joe said. "Can you supervise Paisley and talk to me at the same time?"

"Sure."

"I was thinking that since I have today off and it's our anniversary, maybe we could all go out for lunch somewhere nice, maybe The Old Train Station?"

"That sounds nice," Stacey answered. "I've been wanting to go there, but I'm not sure about Paisley's table manners. You know what happened last time I took her to lunch."

Joe nodded. "But it's been a couple of months since then, and she won't learn how to act in public unless we teach her."

"Okay, you don't have to sell me on some time away from home, honey. I think they have brunch from ten to twelve o'clock, and Paisley usually naps around one, so it would work out fine," Stacey said with a smile. "Oops, Paisley, in your mouth, not on the floor." She rolled her eyes at Joe, who just laughed.

"Don't worry - nobody will pay us any attention."

The Mullen family arrived at The Old Train Station at ten-fifteen. Joe and Stacey had eaten just some toast and juice early, so they were ready for brunch. By the time they were situated, it was ten-thirty. Stacey had perused the buffet as they entered.

"Why don't you go first, Joe? I'll watch Paisley, then we'll swap."

That is what they did. Paisley did well with plain scrambled eggs and a little oatmeal. Stacey stayed away from high-sodium food like bacon or sausage, but there were plenty of choices for her. They had a pleasant experience, Paisley was good, and they enjoyed some small talk.

"Looks like we got here just in time; it's started to rain," Stacey said as she looked out the window.

"Hopefully it will blow over soon," he said, frowning. Their car wasn't particularly close to the door and they hadn't brought umbrellas.

Stacey jumped. "The baby kicked very hard that time. I think he's getting bored, tired of waiting. Hold on, sweetheart, only two more months to go," she said to her stomach.

At that moment, everyone in The Old Train Station stopped talking - they had all heard the tornado siren.

"Run, Stacey!" Joe hollered. "Get in the car. I'll carry Paisley!"

Everyone in the restaurant had the same idea, and the doors were suddenly crammed with people trying to exit the train cars - they were shouting, pushing and shoving. As Stacey reached the front door, she was slammed into the door jamb and cried out, but Joe didn't hear her over the din, and continued to run to the car with his daughter. Halfway there, he turned around and saw Stacey doubled over just outside the train.

Joe ran back to his wife, fighting against the crowd. Holding Paisley with one arm he assisted Stacey to their car. He opened the door and put Paisley inside, then as quickly as possible helped Stacey in. By this time, the rain was coming down hard and fast, with lightning and thunder to match. He got in and started the car, but they were facing into the wind and rain pummeled the windshield making it impossible for Joe to see. The car rocked and Stacey gasped. Joe decided to drive backwards looking out the rear window through the lot until he reached the exit, then turned towards home. In just a few minutes he'd nearly reached their driveway. Pressing the clicker, he opened the garage door, but unfortunately he hit the curb with a tire, causing the car to jolt under the passenger seat.

Stacey, who had been very quiet till now, cried out in pain. Once in the garage, Joe closed the garage door and helped Stacey out. Their walk-in storm shelter was in the garage. Joe gathered Paisley into his arms and guided Stacey to the shelter. It was there, on a chaise lounge in a 6'x6' tornado shelter, that Stacey brought Robin into the world.

Just before the Mullens family arrived for brunch, Jake Ezel had dropped by The Old Train Station to pick up his paycheck. Checks were held in the gift shop, so that was where Jake was when the siren began to sound.

The pretty cashier who had been flirting with Jake for a moment startled, eyes opening wide. "Is that the tornado siren?" Everyone in the gift shop heard it as well.

"Where is the nearest shelter?" Jake asked with a calmness he didn't recognize.

"We don't have one. This is a real train on railroad tracks," she answered nervously, watching the customers begin to panic.

Jake thought fast. He remembered reading that ditches were dug alongside train tracks to drain water away away from the tracks and prevent them from corroding over time. There were at least a dozen people in the gift shop, plus many customers and staff in the dining cars, and they all had to move quickly.

"Everybody, leave right now and lay down in the ditch along the track. Don't push, just do it as fast as possible. Go, go, go!" he yelled above the excited voices.

While everybody in the gift shop left, Jake entered one dining car and repeated his message. But the short delay in getting to the first car had given the diners and staff time to panic, and there was much commotion. He glanced at the sky and saw with horror a funnel cloud developing perhaps a mile away. It was raining heavily now; there wasn't much time. Some people had managed to drive away and he wished them luck in avoiding the tornado. Jake directed as many people as he could to the deep ditches on both sides of the train track. "Stay there and don't leave!" he kept yelling above the din of voices and the rumble of thunder. When he was sure nobody was left on the train, he jumped into a ditch himself and began to pray for the lives of all. How ironic, he thought, to finally understand what it meant to be of service to people.

-26-

Dean Spreads the Word

Something had been troubling me about Dublin, something to do with the weather. Janet thought we might go on a trip today; she's been wanting to see the fjords and northern lights in Norway, but I didn't feel I should leave just yet. I begged off and went to find Willard Scott, legendary television weatherman, for some advice.

After he passed, it hadn't taken long for Willard to resume his career as an entertainer. I found him sitting in a circle with young souls, telling stories and making funny faces. His aura was bright with loving kindness as he sang songs and made appropriate noises according to the tales he told.

At some point, he saw me standing off to the side, and waved.

"Come on over, sit down and sing along!" he said to me.

"I can't sing, never could," I said, shaking my head.

"You might be surprised," he answered as he began singing with the little ones, "There was a farmer who had a dog and Bingo was his name-o."

As I joined in with "B-I-N-G-O", I was delighted I could finally sing in tune, but that wasn't why I was there.

When the song was over and the little ones returned to others' care, I introduced myself to Willard, telling him I was a big fan of his over the years. Yes, even such as I could be a fan - everyone needed to know the weather, especially those who lived in farm country.

He thanked me, and I told him why I'd searched him out.

"Mr. Scott ..." I began.

"Willard," he insisted.

"Willard, this may sound odd to you, but again, nothing here is odd, just temporarily unexplained. Anyway, I've been visiting my hometown regularly since I passed, and today I had the oddest feeling there was something big coming, something to do with the weather. It's the end of spring and Dublin, Tennessee - that's my town - normally does have erratic weather about now, but this feels much different. I'm concerned, should I be?"

Instead of answering right away, he focused his senses both up and down (again, figuratively speaking), and finally said, "Very bad thunderstorms and probable tornadic winds are developing near your town, Dean. I don't know why the intensity of the storms hasn't been detected, but they're coming soon."

Willard's serious demeanor made me tremble for my fellow Dubliners.

"Is there anything I can do?" I asked.

"Warn them to take precautions," he advised.

"But not everybody can see or hear me," I answered.

"Tell those who can," he advised again. "I'll help you."

"Yes!" I said, "I know a few people who are sensitive - I'll start with them. And I'll tell you about a few others who can spread the word. And my wife, Janet, will give it a go - I know she will."

"There's no time to lose, Dean. Let's tell Janet and get started."

We all spread out in Dublin; I headed immediately for Father McCarthy, hoping he was at Saint Isidore's. I know he'd seen me at Don Ryan's funeral, and he could contact a great many people through social media. I hoped he wouldn't faint again when he saw me as there was little time to waste. Yes, there he was at his desk, working on his Sunday sermon. That was great - at least he was sitting down. I let my voice begin first.

"Father McCarthy?"

He looked towards the door and saw nobody. "Father McCarthy, this is Dean Brennan speaking."

His eyes widened and his back straightened, but before he stood up, I brought my spirit body into view. "Please don't be afraid of me. I have something very important to tell you."

"Dean Brennan?" he whispered. "Yes, then I'm not going crazy, thank goodness."

"Father, I'm here to warn you that a violent storm is on its way."

"Yes, the weatherman said there would be thunderstorms today."

"What he doesn't know and didn't say is there will be a tornado, perhaps a few, heading straight for Dublin. You must get the word out for people to take precautions immediately."

Father McCarthy hesitated a moment. "I can text the parishioners as a group, but why would they believe me? I'm not a meteorologist, just a simple priest."

"Tell them an angel spoke to you (I almost laughed when I said that, but didn't) and told you to warn everybody. Tornadoes are very unpredictable and can form quickly. It's a matter of life or death. There's little time to waste!"

I was speaking with such urgency that I could feel my energy waning. Needing to conserve some for several others, I faded out, but not before I saw the good priest cross himself as he picked up his cell phone.

Next, I found Mayor Beau Ryan in his office, on the phone. Before I said anything, I looked around for a few seconds. This used to be my office, a somewhat austere and magisterial room, I'm embarrassed to say. Now, it was a comfortable room with overstuffed country-style chairs and a loveseat in medium-gray, *and Beau's pecan desk, file cabinet, credenza, and bookshelf from his office at Ryan and Ryan. Back to business.*

The phone call sounded more personal than business-like, so I said, "Hello, Beau, this is Dean Brennan". I stood pretty close to him, so I knew he heard me.

"Ah, excuse me, dear, I have another call coming in. I'll be home in time for dinner, bye," he said, then hung up the phone and sat stock still, hands on his desktop. "Dean?" he asked.

"I'm right here, Beau. Sorry if I've startled you, but I have something very urgent to tell you."

"Where are you?" Beau asked.

I apparated next to him. He jumped a little but didn't take his eyes off me.

"I see you, Dean. What's going on?" To his credit, Beau sounded calm, not frightened.

"I don't have a lot of time or enough energy to explain everything, but please believe me when I tell you the predicted thunderstorms will spawn at least one, maybe more, tornadoes this morning. Dubliners need to prepare immediately."

"How do you know this?" he asked with caution. I actually appreciated that; it meant he was paying attention.

"First, I sensed it; then I followed up with the best meteorologist I know, and he told me I was right. You need to spread the word, Beau. You're the mayor - everyone will listen to you. Don't delay."

"What time?" he asked, his face serious.

"Late morning." I flickered and he noticed.

"I'll take care of it," Beau promised. "I'm grateful for the warning. If a tornado doesn't touch down here, I'll just be

embarrassed, but if it does, you'll have helped save many lives. So long, Dean. Say hi to Dad for me."

I tried to answer, but I had faded away. I had more people to tell and hoped I could rally my energy again. If I was lucky, they'd be together.

Old Mrs. Morningsong and her husband Enoli were harvesting vegetables in the garden behind their house. It was drizzling and cloudy so they were rushing. I tried to apparate, but my energy was low. "Excuse me, Didanawisgi, I am former Mayor Dean Brennan. Do you remember me?"

Enoli set his basket on the ground and straightened. "I hear you, Mayor Brennan. How can I help you?"

"I have a strong feeling there's very bad weather coming our way - a tornado, possibly more than one."

Enoli closed his eyes and breathed in deeply, then frowned. "I should have known," he admonished himself. "I dreamed of this last night."

"Would you please ask your family to spread the word and find shelter? My source is predicting late morning, only a few hours away. It will happen suddenly."

"Yes, certainly. Awinita and I will begin immediately. And thank you for addressing me as "Healer"."

I would have liked to chat with him about his background as a medicine man, and education in the western medical system, but I had to muster nearly all my strength to answer. "You're welcome, doctor. I'll be in touch", and I poofed away to recharge my batteries..

-27-

Quentin Flatbush

Quentin Flatbush sat on his soft leather recliner, staring out the window with a can of Bud Light in one hand and the TV remote in the other. The television wasn't on, the can was empty, and the house was quiet as usual. Rarely was Quentin in a pensive mood, as his several businesses kept him busy. He enjoyed the hustle and bustle of Mom's Bakery. Under the supervision of Erline Tessenholtz (who referred to herself as an escapee from the northeast) for the past twenty-five years, Mom's produced delectables for Dublin's residents, restaurants, and businesses all over the city.

He enjoyed watching the constant flow of customers in and out of Fresh Street Market, too. The former N. Vogel Groceries had benefitted when a chain supermarket left town, leaving Dublin with a friendly, yet complete, shopping experience. Ching-ching!

Flatbush Gas & Auto Repair, lay at the end of Broad Street near the cemetery. Under the supervision of Tony DiMarco, the business provided a good, steady source of income and required little of his personal day-to-day attention. He trusted Tony and his mechanics to treat their customers well. He'd surely hear about it if they didn't.

And his newest venture, Dublin Xpress Pharmacy, was finally turning a profit since a competitive pharmacy closed, leaving an empty building on a very good corner; perhaps he should look into that some day.

In his spare time, he acted as one of Dublin's three city aldermen. He had worked hard all his life and enjoyed his successes and the status of being one of the city's leading citizens.

Usually Quentin appreciated being alone in his quiet home, but tonight something was on his mind. He put down the remote and empty beer can and went to the dining room table where he had left an old photo album. Smiling faces, shy smiles, funny grins and crossed eyes, poses that nobody assumed unless they were being photographed, old vehicles, fragile young trees now grown tall and strong, dusty tracks where there were now paved roads; many of these photographs depicted a time before Dublin had even a thousand residents.

Turning a page, his eyes fell on the photograph of a lovely young woman with thick, dark hair and laughing eyes. He couldn't help but smile as he gazed at the image. Her name was Colleen O'Leary, the only woman he had ever loved.

Quentin was twenty-one when he met Colleen on an autumn hayride. Well, technically, off the hayride, as he'd somehow managed to slide down two bales of hay onto the ground when one of the wagon's wheels thumped over a boulder. As he sat there embarrassed, a face floated into view.

"Are you hurt?"the beauty asked, her forehead furrowed with concern.

"Just my pride," he half-joked. "I've never fallen off the wagon before."

Were her eyes brown or hazel? It was hard to tell in the moonlight, but her smile brightened the night.

"Perhaps you should get off the cold ground," she advised. "Do you need a hand?"

He shook his head, rose, and dusted himself off. "I'm Quentin Flatbush," he said.

"My name is Colleen O'Leary", she answered with a soft Irish lilt. "I must say, I don't have men throwing themselves at my feet every day."

Quentin smiled at her Irish wit. "I'm surprised, Miss O'Leary. I'd have thought it happens quite often."

A voice from the wagon, which had stopped, called out, "Quentin, are you coming?"

"No, go on without me," he answered, waving them on. He'd rather stay with the woman with whom he had literally fallen in love.

"I need to find her!" Quentin exclaimed, his fervor heightened by two cans of beer. "I won't live the rest of my life not knowing what happened, even if I have to talk to every O'Leary in the region, or fly to the ends of the earth!"

At work the following morning, Quentin asked his assistant to hold his calls, then searched the internet for private investigators. He spoke with several before choosing Evelyn Key, who had worked twenty-five years with the Tennessee Bureau of Investigation before going into solo practice. She agreed to meet with him at his office that afternoon to assess the case and explain payment for services rendered. She arrived at two o'clock precisely and was ushered into Quentin's office by his assistant.

"Ms. Key, so glad to meet you," Quentin said, rising to shake hands.

"Likewise," she stated, returning his firm grip. She seemed a no-nonsense kind of person, middle-aged, dressed in a business suit, and wearing what older people call "sensible shoes". She sat down before Quentin directed her, then opened her small pocketbook and handed him a business card. "You'll see there are several ways to reach me," she said, "but I do stay in close touch with my clients during a case. Now, what can I do for you, Mr. Flatbush?"

Back in his chair, Quentin felt slightly intimidated by this woman, but was satisfied he'd chosen the right person for the job. "Ms. Key, I would like to hire you to find someone for me. We were married many years ago, then she suddenly disappeared, and I haven't heard from her since. I don't know whether she's still alive, although I've never seen an obituary in any of our local newspapers or online. Can you find her for me?"

"I've located many missing people, Mr. Flatbush," she assured him. "If you'll provide me with dates, names, and any information you feel is pertinent, I will come up with an answer. Hopefully, a positive one."

They spent the next hour discussing the sudden disappearance of Colleen O'Leary Flatbush, and Evelyn Key's rates and expenses. By the end of that hour, Quentin's heart was lighter. As he walked her to the office door, he knew without a shadow of a doubt she would find his Colleen.

<h1 style="text-align:center">-28-</h1>

<h2 style="text-align:center">Colleen's Story</h2>

Despite daily phone calls to and from Private Investigator Evelyn Key, and although she assured him it wouldn't be much longer until the final piece of the puzzle clicked into place, Quentin had his concerns. Why was it taking so long? But then again, since he had waited so many - too many - years to initiate the search, he should be able to wait a little longer. He kept busy with his businesses and made some phone calls regarding his alderman responsibilities. Still, in the back of his mind he constantly wondered how Ms. Key was doing.

Finally, she called him early one morning. "I have excellent news for you, Mr. Flatbush. I found Colleen."

At last, the words he'd been waiting to hear. "Thank you! Where is she?"

"She's right here," Ms. Key said, laughing. "She's dying to talk to you, so I'm handing over the phone."

"Hello, hello, Quentin?" Colleen asked, as if she wasn't sure who she was speaking with.

"Colleen! Yes, it's me. Is that really you? I can hardly believe it! Where are you?"

"I'm in Memphis, darling," she answered. "And you're still in Dublin according to this lovely lady. Oh, I so want to see you!"

"You're only five hours away, sweetheart. Give me your address and be there as soon as I can!"

That afternoon, after his frantic drive to Memphis, and a warning from a Tennessee Highway Patrolman, Quentin and Colleen sat close together on her couch, holding hands, smiling at each other. In fact, they really hadn't said very much yet, not wanting to break the spell, and finding comfort in each other's presence and warm kisses.

"My face hurts from so much smiling," Colleen said, her Irish lilt still charmingly perceptible.

"If I kiss it again, will that help?" Quentin murmured in her ear.

She nodded, then sighed. "We have so much to catch up on. It's been a long time."

"Thirty seven years and two months," he said, "but who's counting?"

She laughed. "Still the wit I see. Well, I suppose I should start first, considering it was me who disappeared." She patted his hand and looked into his eyes. It's a rather sad story, I'm afraid."

"I'm listening."

"My parents, as you know, were strict Catholics. We went to church several times a week and did everything according to church custom. The children were supposed to marry within our faith, raise the children as Catholics, and continue the lineage. We rarely interacted with non-Catholics except when necessary, such as when we went shopping. The day you and I met, I'd been accompanied by two of my brothers. But they were occupied with looking at some girls in another direction when you slid off the wagon, which is the only reason I had one minute to talk to you at all."

"Thank you, young ladies, wherever you are," Quentin said gently.

"Yes. Well, you recall how secretive we had to be in order to see each other after that, and then we rashly decided to defy my parents by getting married by a Justice of the Peace. They were furious when I told them I'd gotten married to a non-Catholic man and planned to move out of the house."

"I thought we agreed to tell them together," Quentin said.

Colleen bowed her head. "I was feeling like a grown up, a married woman now. But my father yelled so loudly he woke the neighbors. My mother found it very hard to look at me, she was so ashamed. Finally, after talking with the priest, my father had our marriage annulled since, at seventeen, I wasn't old enough to marry without their consent. That evening I had one hour to pack my bags as I was to go live with my uncle and his family in Memphis. We left Dublin in the middle of the night because he didn't want the neighbors to see me moving out."

Colleen paused a moment to take a deep breath. Quentin said nothing, but continued to study her face.

"I was miserable in Memphis. Under my father's orders, I was forbidden to use the phone unless a member of the family listened in, lest I call you. I couldn't write a letter to you, either. But the worst was wondering if you were all right, if you hated me for leaving you without a word. I was afraid all the time - for you and for me. There was no way out of the situation but to remarry in order to leave my uncle's house. After a few years, when I was twenty, I met a nice man at church. Paul Patterson was an architect, just a few years older than I, but already a junior partner with his firm. He was a very smart, good- looking Catholic, albeit not as strict as my family. We were married and had five children, and were happy. Paul passed away almost a year ago. I miss him terribly and pray for him every day. But, Quentin, I never forgot you. Never. I prayed you were alive and well for all these years. I asked my priest if I was committing a sin to be so concerned about our very brief, unconsummated marriage when I was very young, and he said it was a venial sin."

"What is a venial sin?" he asked.

"A venial sin can be forgiven with prayers, the canon, and communion. I did all those things many times over - and now, here you are. It's a miracle," she said, gazing into his eyes.

"I never forgot you either," Quentin said. "For the life of me, I wanted to; I tried, but I couldn't. I called every O'Leary for miles around, but they all denied knowing you, or they never let on."

"Quentin, what about your family? I remember you mentioning your parents and sister. Did you tell them about our marriage?" Colleen asked quietly.

"Yes, I did," he admitted. "They were surprised, obviously, but my parents married young, so they understood. After you were gone, we were all confused. I considered myself married until hearing otherwise. My mother, in particular, was saddened by not having grandchildren to carry on the Flatbush name."

"Oh, Quentin," she said sadly, "it hurts to know you never gave yourself permission to remarry. What must you have thought of me?"

"It's all right, love," he said, stroking her hair. "I resolved myself to a life of bachelorhood while searching for you. I worked with my father in our grocery store, and started branching out into business, learning as I went along and taking some college courses when I could. It's been an interesting life, and I don't regret anything except for not having you by my side."

Quentin took Colleen's face gently in his hands and kissed her again. They had to make up for lost time.

-29-

Tornado!

On the second day the Nunezes planned to visit the campground, the weather was cooler and gray. The wind was strong, aggressively pushing the clouds across the sky. Rachel Nunez expressed her concern to Fiona O'Mooney.

"Good morning, Mrs. O'Mooney," she said when she and Lucas went down to breakfast. "Have you heard the weather forecast for today? We're supposed to visit the campground, but my cell phone is calling for strong winds and rain."

"Good morning, Mrs. Nunez," Fiona answered, wiping her hands on her apron. "To be honest, I haven't turned the TV weather on yet. We had a little incident in the kitchen that kept us busy for an hour or so."

As if on cue, Curly Pete came out of the kitchen with a sink aerator hose in his hand; his shirt and pants were wet. "I finally got it off, Mrs. O," he said. "Izzy will run to the hardware store for a new one, and I'll call my brother Billy to install it, if that's ok with you."

"That's good, Pete, please call him. I also know you keep a change of clothes here, so go dry yourself off and I'll take over for Izzy while he's gone," Fiona said.

Overhearing this conversation, Lucas was clearly disappointed. "If Izzy has to run an errand, we'll get there late."

Rachel put her hands on her son's shoulders. "Lucas, we're really not in a hurry, and it's Izzy's job to help everyone at the B&B. He'll take us when he gets back."

139

Lucas nodded his head, resigned. "Well, I'm hungry. I'm going to make another one of those waffles with strawberries and whipped cream. And some bacon, too."

"Let's go, then," Rachel said, and wheeled him to the dining room which was filling up with hungry guests.

In the meantime, Izzy was mentally restructuring his morning. First, he had to drive to the hardware store, return to the Morning Glory with the part, then pick up the van at Jason Ford Realty. They'd get to the campground not too much later than planned. Not only was Izzy's day starting out busy, but it would be memorable, as well.

After they'd eaten and the breakfast crowd broke up, the Nunezes went back to their room to get ready for their day trip. Lucas re-inspected his pack, making sure he had his binoculars, sunglasses, trail maps, and various other necessities. Rachel, who would be walking the trails, made sure to wear her comfortable sneakers again. She also packed bug repellant, sun block, an umbrella, her cell phone, and two bottles of water.

"Do we have time to visit the cats?" Lucas asked.

"I don't think so. Let's just wait in the lobby. We don't want to hold Izzy up when he gets back. Besides, the cats aren't going anywhere - you can see them when Ellie comes to feed them this afternoon."

"You're right, I guess."

Izzy returned to the B&B by 9:30 with the van, and they were soon underway. Lucas chattered the whole time it took to drive to the campground, but Rachel kept looking at the sky. She didn't like what she saw, and the pit of her stomach was speaking to her. Izzy agreed it might rain, maybe a strong cell would roll through, but that was part of living in eastern

Tennessee, and there were many shelters throughout the campground. He told them Trey Monroe knew where they were - all employees did in order to ensure the safety of their guests.

Trey met the van when they pulled into the parking lot nearest the nature trails. He put them at ease right away with his local drawl and easy smile as everyone introduced themselves. "It's nice to meet y'all," he said to Izzy and the Nunezes. "How old are you, son? I think my twins are about your age."

"I'm eleven, twelve soon." Lucas answered. "The cast will be coming off around my birthday, and I can't wait."

"I'm sure that's right. Well, I work in the Maintenance Department, but I helped develop the nature trails and I'm proud of that. They turned out great, so let's get started before it rains," Trey said. "But don't worry, Mrs. Nunez, there are several shelters along the trails to sit out the rain and so on. Would you like me to push your wheelchair, Lucas? Give Mom a break?"

"Yes, push please," Lucas agreed. "Mom can take more pictures if her hands are free."

"That's true," said Rachel. "All right, guys, let's go. Thank you, Izzy, and I guess we'll see you at two o'clock?"

"Yes, ma'am," he said. He needed to get back pretty soon as some B&B guests were scheduled to come and go, and his services were needed as bellman. He also spelled Rosemary on the front desk during her lunch break, and checked on the cats several times a day. Izzy often thought of himself as Cinderella, running from the attic to the basement at the same time, but he enjoyed working at the Morning Glory. He was never bored, that was for sure!

Trey and the Nunezes headed for the wheelchair accessible trail. This was the first time Trey had an opportunity to experience it while pushing a wheelchair. The concrete walkway made for an easy ride, and it was wide enough for others to pass without crowding someone off the path. He'd checked it earlier for poison ivy or nettles. There were no poison sumac or oak trees along the trails, having been taken care of by professional landscapers, but you couldn't be too careful.

They'd only been walking a few minutes when they felt a few raindrops. Rachel brought out her umbrella in case it worsened.

"We can handle a little rain, can't we, Mom?" asked Lucas. He wasn't going to turn around now they were already on the trail.

"I wouldn't worry about it," Trey agreed, although the drops were picking up.

But Rachel's gut feelings were different. What if it started to thunder? Lucas's cast was plastic, and he had a tarp. But thunder was different, not to mention lightning which had struck and splintered the old tree at The Morning Glory just days ago. "Let's get to the first shelter and wait a little while to see if it blows over like Izzy thought," she said, mostly to calm herself down.

"That's fine," Trey said. "The first one isn't far ahead."

Rachel gripped her umbrella like a talisman against the rain. She couldn't help feeling foolish, but she was still mourning her beloved Tomas, and couldn't stand the thought of anything harming her only child.

They stepped up their pace, although Lucas complained they were going too fast - he was going to miss something for sure. Nonetheless, he was glad to see the little log cabin shelter a hundred yards ahead as the skies burst open and the rain began coming down hard. The wind picked up, too, bending the surrounding foliage to and fro. It pushed under the wooden door and howled through the trees. However, they felt safe in the sturdy little shelter, waiting for the storm cell to blow through, wondering how many people had been caught in the downpour before they could run inside.

After fifteen minutes, the rain let up and the wind abated. "See?" Trey said with a grin. "It was just a little Tennessee rain - no biggie." He thought of Amanda and her little charges, including three of his own children, safe and dry inside the daycare center.

Lucas wanted to continue on the trail; he hadn't seen any deer or other "critters" yet, and they hadn't taken many photos, so they left the little cabin, closed the door securely, and continued on the path.

For the next twenty minutes, there was a cooling breeze for which they were grateful as the sun was now overhead. Even though the trail cut through the forest, the sun could reach them. Rachel took photos of some of the beautiful wildflowers they passed along the way, and when they caught sight of a family of deer, she carefully got a few good snaps of them before they turned and walked away.

"That was great, Mom!" Lucas said. "That one deer had some horns on its head."

"That was a buck, Lucas," Trey replied. "He's growing his antlers for the fall when he has to fight all the other bucks. He'll shed them in October after the rutting season is over."

"Rutting?" Lucas asked. "Why does he have to fight?"

"Um, your Mom will answer that one - one day," Trey grinned.

Suddenly, the wind picked up again and the temperature dropped a few degrees. "Dang, it's going to rain again," Trey said, "and we're in-between shelters." As his Walkie-Talkie began sending an emergency alert, he heard something that sent a chill down his spine. The tornado siren in Dublin had begun to sound. Trey looked at Rachel; she knew what she heard and her eyes grew round with fear.

"Let's run for it," Trey said as calmly as possible so as not to frighten Lucas, too. "Hold on, Lucas. We're going to the next shelter."

Rachel followed them as fast as she could run without letting Lucas out of her sight. She wasn't used to running, though, and started lagging behind. Trey kept going while pushing Lucas's wheelchair. He would come back for her when he got Lucas to the shelter. The rain was pelting them now with large, cold drops, while the temperature continued to drop. The siren continued its warning. When the first crack of lightning lit the sky, followed closely by a thunderous boom, Lucas screamed. Trey could see the shelter ahead and rallied his strength to get the boy inside as soon as possible. As he opened the door, another thunderclap sent Lucas into a panic. He tried to get out of his wheelchair, even though there was nowhere else to go. Trey grabbed the boy and told him to sit tight, that he was going back to get his mother and bring her to the shelter. Wild-eyed, Lucas only knew he'd be alone in this place by himself, surrounded by his worst nightmare. But Trey had no options - he had to leave the boy alone for a few minutes to help Mrs. Nunez; she couldn't be that far away.

Trey opened the door with great effort as the wind was blowing against it, and jogged down the trail, trying to see Rachel in the pouring rain. In a hundred yards he saw her, bent over with her hand on her side, crying. "I can't run anymore - I have a stitch in my side and leg cramps," she said. "Just go back to Lucas - I'll be there as soon as I can."

"I can't leave you out here alone," Trey yelled over the din. "We'll take it slow. Just keep walking."

Rachel said nothing; she couldn't do much more than follow his lead. When another lightning bolt lit the sky followed by a thunderclap, she managed to yell, "My son is terrified of thunderstorms!"

"He's safe," Trey said, hoping he was right. In the back of his mind, though, were his wife and children in the daycare center. Were THEY safe? He began to whisper, "Dear Lord, give me the strength to help these people and dispel our fears." As if in answer to his prayer, the little shelter came into view.

"Look!" he hollered to Rachel, "there's the shelter! See, we made it and everyone will be fine."

They stumbled into the cabin, soaked to the skin, shivering with cold. The noise outside was blocked only a little by the thick walls. Rachel ran to Lucas who was crying and trembling, and pulled him close to her.

"Oh, Lucas, you're safe - we're all safe! I love you so much," she murmured over and over.

Trey watched, his wet clothes and hair dripping onto the floor. He knew they weren't really safe yet. Their eardrums and sinuses throbbed with the sound and sensation of a tornado, and as long as they could hear the sirens, there was still a chance of injury, or worse. But he said nothing of this to mother and son. Looking around the little cabin, he found several thick towels in a foot locker that also served as a seat, and handed them around. While he dried his hair, Trey heard a tree crash down nearby and he shuddered. It could have fallen on the shelter and they'd have been crushed; the shelter was little more than a place to run in from the rain. *I could use a drink right now*, he thought, but the memory of Dean's intervention manifested vividly in his mind, and he shook his head to clear it. There was too much at stake to slide backwards again. The tree hadn't fallen on them, and that was good enough for now.

Don Ryan and I looked at the tall pine that would surely have flattened the little shelter and its occupants. The rain and wind had no effect on us, of course, but I couldn't suppress a shiver.

"I couldn't have done it without you, Don," I said, throwing my arm around my friend's shoulders. "That pine was bigger than I thought it was at first."

"I was glad to help," Don answered. "Thanks for calling me. And by the way, Dean, thanks for all the support you gave me at my funeral. I wasn't afraid, just confused by the changes."

"That's good to hear," I said. "Let's check in with these folks quickly, then survey the area. Maybe there's more we can do for others. Hey, the sirens have stopped- let's go."

Inside the shelter, Lucas was pulling himself together and no longer crying, while Rachel and Trey sat silently waiting for the rain to end; thankfully, it seemed to be passing. They were all grateful they had come through this in one piece, and again, Trey's thoughts went to his family. He had no idea where they were right now, but he prayed wherever they were, they were safe. His ankle, although healed, was aching; he'd wrenched it while running Lucas's wheelchair down the trail. Eventually he'd have to check with the doctor, but the ache in his heart was worse.

"Mrs. Nunez, I'm worried about my family," he said quietly so Lucas couldn't hear. "I have a wife and seven children, and don't know where they all are right now. Are you up to leaving even though it's still raining? Or would you rather wait it out without me? The wind has died down and I don't hear the sirens anymore."

"Dios mio!" she whispered. "Such a big family! Of course we can continue. We can't be far from the parking lot, surely." She glanced at Lucas. "I'll ask my son."

Lucas looked at his mother. "I heard, Mom. If you're up to pushing, I'm ready to go. We have to find Mr. Monroe's family and make sure they're okay."

Trey clapped Lucas lightly on the shoulder. "Thanks, son, that's kind of you. We're only a couple of minutes from the parking lot, so let's go."

When the threesome opened the door, Mrs. Nunez gasped. "The tree, look at the tree!"

It was hard to miss; the old pine had fallen from the opposite side of the path, landing just a few feet from the cabin's side. Lucas's eyes grew wide, and he whispered, "Let's get out of here."

Fortunately, there were no major obstructions on their way to the trailhead, although they saw evidence that a tornado had passed through. A wide swath of field thistles and wildflowers looked as if someone had driven a bulldozer in a straight line to the lake. Trey hoped and prayed nobody had been out boating or sailing when the storm began to brew.

The sky was beginning to clear in the west; the sun shining through the clouds glowed an eerie green and purple, the result of dirt and dust rising into the air. The threesome drove purposefully to the childcare center, avoiding fallen tree limbs, waste receptacles, and other items strewn about. Trey was gripping the wheel so tightly the ligaments stood out on his forearms. They hadn't seen anybody out in the few minutes it had taken them to reach the front where the childcare center and check-in/information building were. The buildings appeared unaffected by the storm, although a lawn chair was caught on the flagpole at the entrance.

Rachel said, "I'll get Lucas out of the van, Mr. Monroe. You go check on your family."

Feeling as if he was running in slow motion, Trey entered the building and hollered, "Hello! Is anybody here? Hello! Where is everyone?"

For a moment he heard nothing and fear gripped his chest. Willing himself to keep breathing, he worked his way into the next room, and remembered the basement shelter he'd been told about during his orientation. Spotting the word 'SHELTER' painted on the wall in bright red, he ran over and lifted the trap door. Once opened, a chorus of voices, young and old, met his ears. "Is it over? I'm scared! What happened?" Then he heard "Trey!" When he descended into the basement, Amanda flew into his arms. They held each other tightly until the other daycare worker and parents who happened to be there when the sirens began, climbed the stairs to make sure it was safe for the children to leave the shelter.

Trey told them, "It's all right. There was a tornado, but it missed these buildings up here. The kids can come up."

"Help me with the little ones," Amanda said. "Fortunately, two of them slept through the whole thing, so they'll be fine. But all the rest of us need to calm down."

Trey nodded his head. "Where are our older ones?"

As Amanda picked up two babies to bring them upstairs, she whispered, "I hope they were still at the B&B and didn't go home after Ellie fed the cats. I tried to call them there, but I couldn't get through." Her eyes brimmed with tears as she stepped out of the basement.

"Amanda, I need to check around to make sure nobody's been hurt. It's part of my job, and we all carry Walkie-Talkies. But as soon as I can get away, I'll find the kids, don't worry. I promise."

"We'll be fine now," Amanda said with a little smile. "In my heart, I know they're safe, too. You do what you need to do; hopefully, nobody was hurt." Trey answered her with a kiss, and left.

Rachel and Lucas had watched this interaction and, for a moment, Rachel choked up thinking about her own husband. She felt Tomas would have done the same thing. Lucas looked up at her, knowing what she was thinking.

Rachel walked over to where Amanda was putting the babies into their cribs. "Your husband is a fine man," she said. "He saved our lives on the trail and kept us calm."

Amanda smiled at her. "Yes, he is a fine man. He certainly is."

As Trey drove the van slowly around the campground, more people were venturing out of the shelters. He asked them if they, or anyone else, needed assistance. One man had tripped over a fallen limb and twisted his knee; Trey requested medical assistance for him via his walkie talkie. Other workers were calling in similar reports, all relatively minor injuries, until Clay Baker requested an ambulance at the cabin area where a woman had suffered a bad accident.

-30-

Beginning and Ending

When Colleen woke the morning after she and Quentin were reunited, she was almost shocked to discover him there beside her for the first time in thirty-seven years. So it wasn't a dream, she thought as she watched him sleep. His face had changed with age; it was a bit heavier, there were a few wrinkles, and was that a scar on his forehead? His black hair was handsomely streaked with gray. But it was the man, not the wrinkles and gray hair she was still in love with for all these years.

She had loved Paul very much; he had given her five wonderful children, security, and all his heart. Yet somewhere in the deep recesses of her being, she had thought of Quentin almost daily, wondering how he was and if he had moved on as she had. But thinking about him made her feel strangely unfaithful to Paul, and she wouldn't have jeopardized their marriage by trying to find Quentin. A simple phone call to Dublin's city hall would have done the trick, but she couldn't bring herself to do so. Many thoughts flew through her mind as she watched him sleeping with a peaceful smile on his face. It was hard to believe he had remained single while she had five children and several grandchildren. Where would they live if they remarried? She couldn't bear to leave them all, even though it was just a few hours' drive. Would Quentin consider moving to Memphis? They would certainly have to talk about it soon.

With a yawn, Quentin opened his eyes to see his Colleen watching him lovingly. No words were necessary as he took her in his arms again.

The phone rang an hour later, but it went unanswered. "Hi, Mom," the voice said to the answering machine. "It's Lindsey. Are you sleeping in? I know it's only seven, sorry if I woke you. I'm just calling to check on you. Give me a call when you can."

"I can't wait to meet your children," Quentin murmured as the machine clicked off. "I hope they'll like me." He didn't notice Colleen's slight hesitation in answering.

"I'm positive they will adore you in time," she said. "But since they know nothing about you - us - at this moment, we'll have to tell them our story very soon. Our former marriage will shake them. They were all very close to their father, you see."

Quentin nodded. "Do you think we can get them all in one place at one time?"

"I'm not sure, darling," she answered. "Lindsey and her family live a few miles away, but the other four are scattered across the country. I've gotten quite comfortable with Skype and Zoom, although they're not ideal." She looked at Quentin with concern, but he just ran his hand gently through her hair, dividing the tendrils gently with his fingers.

"And I have to return to Dublin today," he said slowly. "As much as I'd like to stay, I need to be at the aldermen's meeting at one o'clock. I'll have to leave right after we have breakfast to make it on time."

"Oh, Quentin, when that nice detective showed up, I never considered how complicated our lives would become. I was so happy - what shall we do?"

"Life is complicated, sweetheart," Quentin said, kissing her forehead. Their lives had gone in different directions, and now that they had the opportunity, he realized it would be impossible to return to the life they had envisioned when they were young, however briefly. "We'll work it out, I'm sure."

When I heard that Quentin had been reunited with his wife, I was as surprised as the next soul. How had he kept that information from me, mister know-it-all? He's always been quiet about his personal life, although I knew his family and about his many business ventures. But married? I guess I never stopped to consider it, as caught up as I was in the world of banking and being the mayor. His work kept him busy, too. Boy, those years went by fast!

I'm curious about their future together. Surely, Colleen doesn't want to move away from Memphis where she's lived for most of her life and raised her family. And I hope Quentin doesn't cash it all in and move away from Dublin, because he's needed here. I guess it's not my decision to make. Whatever they decide is their business; I'll have to wait and see.

Janet just reminded me that we're going to miss Bad Movie Night if I keep dithering. They're playing The Blob, with Steve McQueen. I took her to see it many years ago when we were dating. It's about, ... well, it's about two hours too long, but at least nobody will hear me snoring through it this time.

PS - If you were wondering, I made it through the movie without falling asleep, but that's because there's no such thing as sleep here in the Great Beyond. It wasn't half as bad as I had remembered, though.

In other news, Quentin and Colleen decided to marry and have planned their honeymoon at, of all places, the campground!

Janet laughed about their choice of venue for the honeymoon, since Quentin could certainly have taken her anyplace in the world. But Colleen wanted to return to Dublin to visit her parents' graves, and make amends with her brothers and their families, if possible. Quentin agreed, although he made her promise they would travel at a later time.

Father Shane McCarthy had the honor of marrying them at Saint Isidore the Farmer Catholic Church. Colleen's three brothers did attend, as did their wives and several of their children. Two of Colleen's children also attended, although three of them couldn't make it on such short notice. Janet and I were there, too; I'd missed their first marriage, so I wasn't missing this one. It was a lovely service, and Janet cried.

-31-

Weathering the Storm

At The Morning Glory B&B, the O'Mooneys and their staff were preparing for the potential tornadoes. One of the guests had seen Mayor Ryan on the TV news with an emergency announcement and everyone was on high alert. Guests were relocated to the basement storage area, the B&B staff battened down the hatches, and Fiona made sure everyone was present and accounted for. Hayden was on his way to the sunroom and catio to bring the cats to the basement with everyone else when the kitchen door opened. They'd forgotten that Ellie and her three older siblings usually dropped by a little later in the morning on Saturdays. While Ellie fed and tended to the cats, the three boys helped Hayden with a few chores to make a little money, too. So when the children showed up, Hayden quickly updated them on what was happening and hustled them downstairs. All except Ellie - she had to know where Oreo and Callie were.

"I haven't checked the catio yet, Ellie, but go with your family and I'll bring them down to you."

"I'll go with you, Mr. Hayden," she said. "It's getting blowy, and they might be too scared to come to you."

Hayden would have protested because of the danger to the child, but she was determined, and time was running short. "Okay, let's get this done quickly," he said, picking up his pace as the wind began to howl more loudly.

It was shockingly apparent that the catio was being destroyed by the wind. Screens were gone, glass was broken, and the cats were nowhere in sight. They looked around frantically for a few moments until they heard the siren begin to wail.

"You go in and down to the basement with everyone else," Hayden told her. "I'll look for another minute but that's all the time we have."

"No!" Ellie exclaimed. "They're my friends and I love them. I'll find them, Mr. Hayden!" When she caught a flash of black and white in the corner of her eye, she yelled, "Oreo! Come here!" and the cat leapt into her arms. To their relief, Callie was close behind. Hayden picked her up and they ran for the basement door.

There was very little talking while they heard the roar outside; it seemed to last forever, although it was only a few minutes. Most people huddled together offering encouraging words, but a few just cried in fear. Ellie and her brothers were quiet as they all sat hand-in-hand, thinking of their parents and younger siblings. And their school friends - were they safe? As the tornado passed close to the B&B, they could hear the roar of the wind and debris being thrown against hard surfaces outside. Hayden wondered for just a moment if the garden would be destroyed before returning his attention to the people in his basement.

The tornado passed, but the siren continued to sound as the storm turned towards the lake - and the campground. The group didn't know that at the time, of course; they'd find out later when news stories were aired. But Ellie began to cry when she remembered that Nunezes had planned on spending the day at the campground. She knew Lucas wasn't agile in his wheelchair, and had no idea if and where they would find shelter. Callie snuggled into Ellie's lap and licked her chin.

"I hope you're telling me that Lucas is okay," she whispered. "Maybe an angel saved him."

She was almost right; two angels had been on guard that day.

The storm passed in less than five minutes. When they could no longer hear the tornado siren, Curly Pete offered to open the basement door. Everyone agreed, anxious to see if there had been damage to the B&B, their vehicles and belongings. He walked up the five cellar steps and turned the doorknob, but there was resistance when he tried to open the door. Izzy and Hayden joined him at the door, but the door wouldn't open more than a few inches. The men looked at each other, reading each other's thoughts. Hayden turned to the dozen people who were watching them with wide-eyed concern.

"It's okay, everybody," Hayden assured them. "We can get out through the window over there," he said, pointing to a corner of the basement. "It was designed as an emergency exit." It was an expense he initially hadn't thought was necessary when they renovated the building, but as it was strongly suggested by the architect, he had relented. Waves of gratitude ran down his spine.

The window was three feet off the floor, so one of the men found a sturdy toolbox to place underneath, then one by one they climbed out into the flower garden, assisting the others. When Hayden lifted Ellie up and out, he gently handed the cats to her and Fiona. He and Curly Pete were the last to leave.

Most of the folks had left to check their cars and rooms, but there was very little talking among the few who stood in the former garden, now a wind-ravaged scene of bent and tangled vines, twigs and branches, broken flower pots and statuary, and flowers on the ground. Fiona looked at Hayden with tears in her eyes and he put his arms around her.

The Monroe children hugged each other with Oreo mashed between them until he wiggled his way out of Ellie's arms to find his sister. Rosemary Zimmer offered them her phone so they could call their parents to let them know they were all right.

"We need to see," Hayden said quietly; Fiona nodded.

To Izzy and Curly Pete he said, "Let's spread out. Why don't you two go around that way, and we'll go this way. Someone may need help."

After walking around the building, it appeared that most of the damage had occurred on the north side where the garden and catio had been. Hayden's art studio in the turret had suffered a broken window due to flying debris, and the studio was a wreck. Rain had poured in, and many of his paintings had been destroyed or damaged. Curly Pete had found the kitchen door wide open, hanging from one hinge. Kitchen utensils were strewn about, the herb garden was destroyed, and the large granite-topped workbench had been blown over onto its side, half of it in front of the basement steps, preventing them from opening the door. Izzy found nearly every vehicle in the parking area had incurred some sort of damage. Only the two-hundred-year-old wooden stump with the new compass on top appeared undamaged.

As they entered the Morning Glory's front door, Hayden and Fiona were surprised to see only a little damage. The reception desk, lobby and dining area seemed intact, despite the large windows in the dining room, and close proximity to the kitchen. Guests who had entered the building after leaving through the basement window wandered around. Some were on their cell phones taking photos and talking with families and insurance agents. But the main house had not sustained much damage inside except for the kitchen, catio, and art studio.

Fiona began to shake and shiver uncontrollably. Hayden put his arm around her and asked, "What's the matter, honey?"

"I'm grateful nobody was hurt and our home is standing. I was so afraid after I saw the morning glory garden that everything would be demolished. We were spared."

"You're right," he said. "Everything's going to be fine." He smiled and kissed her on the cheek. "The flowers will regrow, windows will be repaired, and we have each other."

Right after Don and I kept the tree from falling on that little shelter at the campground, he went to check on Beau and his family, and I went to the B&B. It was hard to maintain the energy needed to do everything I wanted to do, but I managed to deflect some of it, enough at least to keep Hayden, Fiona, and everyone else safe, and prevent the building from being destroyed. Janet went to our other children to make sure they were safe, but she couldn't keep the tornado from destroying our family farm. Fortunately, we heard our eldest son and his wife were at the campground's farm when it came through and they were able to seek shelter with others.

Enoli and Awinita had performed a ceremony shortly before the storm came through which apparently slowed the winds and downgraded it from an F3 to an F2. If they hadn't done that, many more buildings and lives would have been lost in the process. When all was calm again, Janet and I poofed away to rest and recharge our batteries on the ley lines of an ancient Native American mound in the southwest. I can't tell you where it is because the folks living nearby don't want a lot of people there selling and buying souvenirs. Can't blame them.

Anyway, I thought you'd be interested in knowing more about how we helped out during the twister. There may be more of them this season; now we know what to expect.

-32-

Fateful Honeymoon

After their wedding ceremony at Saint Isidore's, the Flatbushes returned to Quentin's house. As he loaded their minimal luggage into the car, Colleen checked the weather with her cell phone. "It looks like we're going to have rain for the next three days, Quentin. They don't predict anything major, just a twenty to thirty percent chance of rain."

"That could be a good thing, you know," he answered, "since it's been so hot this past week. Are you ready to go?"

"Yes, I checked all the locks and watered the indoor plants. The rain should take care of the rest. We're going to have a wonderful time, aren't we? I can't wait to go on the peddleboats or float around the lake on an inner tube. I've missed living near water."

As Quentin opened the passenger door for his new bride, he said, "You surprise me! You lived just a few miles from the Mississippi River, darling. That's considered water."

She laughed. "Well, water I could swim in, let's say. Oh, dear, it's already starting to drizzle."

"Then let's get this honeymoon on the road!"

They checked into their cabin as Mr. and Mrs. Flatbush. Colleen looked at her new wedding ring again, blissfully happy. Quentin beamed at her; finally his dream had come true. They took their time unpacking their few items, listening to the rain gently pattering the windows and the roof.

"Looks like we got inside just in time," he said, looking around at the neat little cabin with its efficient kitchen, two

161

double beds, and comfortable furnishings. "I've always liked to sleep when it's raining," he mused. Then, taking her into his arms, he whispered, "But I don't feel like sleeping, do you?"

The sun rose brightly on day one of their honeymoon, and the Flatbushes decided it would be a good day to rent a peddleboat. After breakfast, they donned their swimsuits and coverups and rode rented bicycles to the lake. Fortunately, there were a few peddleboats left to rent, as Quentin had told Colleen he wasn't very good with canoes and paddles. But the boats were easy to steer, so they rented one for an hour and left the dock. They laughed like children until their legs tired out.

After half an hour or so, Quentin began panting with exertion. "I'm not as young as I used to be," he admitted to Colleen.

"I don't know about that, dear," she said with a wink. She looked at her watch. "Let's just go down to those marker buoys, then turn around and come back."

"Sounds good," he said. Maybe canoeing would have been a better idea, Quentin mused. They'd rent a canoe tomorrow and find out.

Back on shore, they biked around the campground, marveling at the size of some of the camper rigs and big multi-room tents they saw. When Colleen hinted about how wonderful it would be to wander around the country in a self-contained motorhome or campervan, Quentin said, "This is something we've never discussed. Are you part gypsy?"

Colleen laughed. "I don't know, maybe. I was pretty established in Memphis for all those years, so I thought perhaps we could travel around, free as birds."

Quentin's idea of travel tended more towards sightseeing tours or maybe cruises. This was something they'd have to consider some day. He knew nothing about motorhomes, and although he had driven many trucks in his lifetime, a motorhome would be a different experience.

Pedaling around, they enjoyed the sights and sounds of the campground and seeing people from all over, but their legs had given out. It had begun to rain again, too, so they'd grabbed a hot dog at the snack bar, rode back to the front to return their rented bikes, and drove back to their cabin.

By this time, the rain was coming down hard, drumming on the roof and windows. "I'm pretty tired," Quentin said. "Do you mind if I take a nap? We were up early, and I don't think we'll be going anywhere soon, anyway. Tonight I thought we'd drive over to The Old Train Station for a nice dinner. How does that sound, dear?"

"Wonderful!" Collen answered. "I've been wondering about that place. The brochure makes it sound very attractive; they even have a pianist in the evenings. Shall I make a reservation? Then I'll join you in a nap. I'm rather worn out myself."

"Good idea," he said looking out the window, and wondering if the rain would stop soon. He was too tired to check his weather app - he'd do that when he woke up. Quentin took off his shoes and slipped under the duvet Colleen had brought along, feeling snug as a bug.

Colleen's call was brief. "We've got seven o'clock reservations," she said as she removed her shoes as well and crawled under the covers with Quentin. One quick kiss, and both were sound asleep within five minutes, exhausted by fresh air and exercise.

While they slept, the wind whipped up and darker clouds quickly rolled in. Within the hour, tornado sirens began to wail in Dublin, but hard rain drumming on the roof nearly drowned out the warning. A tremendous crack of lightning finally brought Quentin to his feet. The sight of a tornado in the clouds moving towards the campsite filled him with terror and he vigorously shook Colleen's shoulder.

"Colleen, Colleen, wake up! There's a tornado coming and we need to get to a shelter immediately!"

She rose quickly and ran to Quentin's embrace. "Where is the nearest shelter?"

A shelter map posted on the front door of the cabin showed the closest one was just a few hundred feet away. Throwing on their shoes, they wrestled the door open and ran in the direction of the shelter sign, along with many other people, some of whom were screaming and crying. They could see the funnel cloud moving quickly in their direction, and heard the sirens through the roar. Rain blinded them as they ran into the wind, hand-in-hand. The shelter was about fifty feet away when the door slammed shut. Quentin tried his hardest to wrestle it open, but either the wind was blowing it shut, or someone had already latched it. He let go of Colleen's hand to bang on the door with both fists. When someone inside helped him get the door open, he turned his back to grab Colleen but she was gone. Gone!

"Colleen!" he screamed into the roaring air as rain, mud and debris swirled around him.

"We can't keep this door open any longer!" yelled a man from inside. "Come in here now!"

"I can't, not without my wife!" Quentin cried. But the man at the door and another fellow grabbed Quentin and pulled him inside, closing the shelter door.

As the tornado roared and raged outside, Quentin screamed and cried, falling on his knees, unnerving everyone in the shelter more than they already were. Some of the women tried to soothe him, saying she'd probably found another shelter, that it would be over soon and he would find her again. But Quentin was inconsolable. "It's my fault!" he cried. "I let go of her hand!"

Within minutes the sound faded; they could hear only rain and wind.

"I'm going out to find my wife!" Quentin demanded. They couldn't stop him as he unlatched the door and ran outside. There was nobody in sight as he looked frantically up and down the road; he walked blindly, calling her name. Finally, he heard her voice and followed it to a nearby stand of trees. Colleen had her arms wrapped around one of them, crying and sobbing, calling his name. Quentin ran to her and pulled her to his chest, while they both cried with relief upon finding each other again.

"It picked me up off my feet, and dropped me here. I've never been so terrified in my life!"

Quentin could say nothing, but continued to hold her tight until she pulled away a little, laughing. "I can't breathe, Quentin," she said. "I promise I won't blow away again."

Embarrassed, Quentin loosened his grasp. "I'm sorry, dearest. I was so frightened. All the people in the shelter think

I'm a maniac, but I was sure you were gone forever because I let go of your hand."

People started milling around a little as the storm abated and the sirens ceased. Someone noticed Colleen had a large bump forming on her temple and offered to call for a medic. Although Colleen demurred, Quentin thanked the woman for her concern and asked her to make the call; he wasn't carrying his cell phone. The crowd disbursed, and everyone headed back to their cabins or other shelters as it was still raining, but the Flatbushes stayed in place so the paramedics could find them.

But as the emergency van pulled up and three people in uniforms jumped out, Colleen collapsed to the ground.

Quentin was treated for shock at Dublin General Hospital. Reliving the events of the tornado, he thrashed and cried "It was all my fault!" until he received an IV sedative. Paramedics had retrieved Colleen's purse from their cabin and found her address book which included the names and numbers of her children. The ER physician on call had the unenviable task of informing them that their mother had died from an impact on her temple and subsequent brain bleed. There had been no time or way to treat her at the campground, and he was very sorry to convey this information, although he wanted them to know she had died painlessly and quickly.

When Janet and I found out about the death of Quentin's new wife, we were both greatly saddened for him. We know that there's really no death, but Quentin and Colleen's family will grieve deeply; there will be denial, perhaps anger. Who could have believed they would be torn apart for the second time in their lives after a very brief reunion? I'm not an expert on the why of things, and don't pretend to be, but sometimes life on earth seems unfathomable, incomprehensible, even cruel. We have to trust that there is a reason for everything and let it go at that, although it will be a long time until Quentin can let it go, if ever.

-33-

Trey's Commitment

When Trey Monroe walked into the medical building that housed Joe Mullen's office, the sun was beginning to set. He had come directly from work at Fisher's Lake Campground and was tired. He loved his job, but it was mostly outdoors and physical work. Today, six weeks after the tornado struck the campground, the maintenance crew was still cleaning up and making repairs. When the elevator door opened he caught sight of himself in the mirrored wall. "Good grief," he mumbled, "I shoulda brought a comb and a change of clothes". The door slid open as he was attempting to tame his hair with his hands and fingers.

Paloma Hernandez smiled at him from the reception desk. Trey noticed her medical books were open. It was no secret that Paloma was getting a jump on a medical career when things were quiet at the Dublin Healing Center, and Trey was their last patient of the day.

"Hello, Mr. Monroe," she smiled. "Dr. Mullen is in his office and you can go right in."

Joe was at his desk and looked up when Trey entered the room. "I apologize for my appearance," Trey said quickly. "I was working in mud today. They gave me some rubber boots, but the rest of me..." he shrugged and indicated his pants.

"No apology needed," Joe replied, standing to shake Trey's hand. "You should see me after my daughter and I have ice cream. The other night she somehow put chocolate handprints on my back."

168

Trey snorted. "You should see our crew after we've had spaghetti and meatballs."

The men sat down to begin the counseling session. Trey spoke first.

"Joe, I'm not gonna lie. This is the hardest thing I've ever done. I don't like being an adult all the time; sometimes I want to give everything up and not worry about anything. Let someone else take over."

"Give up on your family, Trey? Your job? Your self-esteem? Your health? Have you had a setback?"

"No, no, I haven't taken a drink since I started coming to the AA group. I don't miss being drunk and the hangovers and all. Sometimes I just don't want to live so responsibly. Does that make sense? But I'm not gonna give up on my family and disappoint Amanda, not again," he said, shaking his head. "And I'm not gonna jeopardize the best job I ever had. It's a new way of life and I'm just getting used to it."

Joe nodded his head. "Adulting is hard, especially when you've had no training for it. You know that Julian and I are just a phone call away if you ever find yourself in a crisis. My wife will gladly lend her support as well. Or call the AA hotline. And remember, you can always call your sponsor; you're not alone in your journey. There's always someone for you to talk to."

Trey sat for a moment, silently looking at his hands in his lap. After a moment, he whispered, "I know a young boy whose father died not that long ago in an accident. His mother is a great parent, but she's going through all that grief herself. I think of Lucas sometimes when I have the urge to drink. I don't want my family to be without a father. But I wish Lucas didn't have to be my conscience." A tear rolled down his cheek. He'd stayed in touch with the Nunezes. Lucas sent him photos of his new cat, and Rachel texted a photo of Lucas without the cast on his leg. The boy was all smiles in those pictures, but Trey knew the loss of his father would take a long time to process. No, he would resist alcohol for his family, and for Lucas, too. He had everything to live for.

-34-

EPILOGUE

Dear friends, so much happened in Dublin over the past few years that it is impossible to relate everything to you. When I spoke to Janet about this, she suggested writing an epilogue to fill in the gaps. I said the gaps would practically constitute another book and she laughed at me, saying "just try to keep it brief, Dean". You may as well know I had a tendency to pontificate while in my corporeal body. Not to digress too much, but communication is so much easier in the Hereafter as it's accomplished telepathically. It's instantaneous and you can't tell a lie. When your life is one big lie, like mine was, well, that's quite a lot to contemplate. Anyway, let me briefly fill in some holes for you.

I've enjoyed watching our family members continue to be good people, citizens, and role models. Thank heavens they didn't take after me. They are thriving and pretty happy with their life choices. Jerry (our daughter Bitsy's husband) sold Cut-Ups, their beauty/barbershop, and finally retired, although he still cuts hair at the assisted care facility a few times a week on a volunteer basis because he likes to chit-chat with his old friends.

Daughter Faye and her husband Robert managed to persuade their son Ronnie to get a job, move out of their basement, and get on with life after his divorce. He teaches auto mechanics at Dublin High School now - so far so good.

Our son Greg and his wife Cindy ran the family farm until it was severely damaged by the twister. While they consider their options, they continue to run the campground's little farm as well. Their three children are all pursuing interesting careers, but not in farming. Time will tell what happens with the farm, but I hope they don't sell it to someone who won't respect the land and its history.

Stacey and Joe Mullen are doing well. Paisley is a smart little girl, and she adores her little brother Robin. He had a rough start being born prematurely and having to stay in an incubator for many weeks, but he rallied well. Stacey returned to her job as pastor of Open Arms Unitarian Church where the congregation welcomed her with, well, open arms. She brings both of their little ones with her and the arrangement is working out nicely due to the assistance of a few ladies who help watch the children while she's busy. Joe's work with troubled teens continues to provide a much-needed service. Recently, funds were made available from an anonymous donor to ensure that all kids in need receive counseling despite their financial circumstances. I know the donor, though. He hadn't been a very nice guy, which made it easy for me to blackmail him years ago. That he's using the money repaid from my estate to help kids in need says a lot about him now.

Matthew Boyd and Tallulah Morningsong were indeed married in June. It was an interesting dual celebration, beginning with a beautiful Cherokee wedding prayer followed by a short devotion by Pastor Stacey Mullen, which Janet and I found moving and insightful (well, of course we were there!). They are very much in love and are planning on having a large family. Read into that what you will.

And what can I say about Jake? He saved many lives by remaining calm and using his head. He could just as easily have run for cover himself and not worried about anyone else. Janet says I changed him, but I don't know. I think he's basically a good guy who thought he could lie his way up to Easy Street. But he learned that didn't have to be the case; now he is a respected and admired citizen of Dublin.

Returning for a moment to the twister and the damage it caused, I heard the Monroes' little home was damaged beyond repair. There was, of course, no insurance. However, they were able to build a home large enough to accommodate their family with help from some of the money I returned to the city upon my death, and a loan from the bank. Clay Baker underwrote the loan; it appears he's planning to keep Trey Monroe in his employ for a long time.

A number of businesses on Broad Street were damaged by the storm, including the large and popular antique mall. Most were rebuilt, but a few had to be razed as they were underinsured or the damage was too severe. Dublin's town library, already a hundred years old and in need of renovation, was closed until Quentin Flatbush purchased and donated the lot where a pharmacy had once stood. He had a new library built there - handsome, strong, offering twice as many books, materials, and electronic resources as the old one. A plaque dedicates the building to the memory of his wife, Colleen.

But the old library was not torn down. The Cherokee people from Dublin and surrounding towns purchased the building from the city and renovated it from top to bottom. Lifelike tableaus inside engross visitors in the native culture. An addition was made to the rear of the building and appointed as a trading post where visitors will find authentic Cherokee goods. Owned and operated by members of the extended Morningsong family, the

Dublin branch of the Museum of the Cherokee Indian provides education of all kinds to residents and tourists all year long.

Do you remember the two-hundred-year-old oak that was struck by lightning at the Morning Glory B&B and withstood the tornado that passed through? Izzy's cousin Atohi, who had originally cut down the old tree, fashioned it into a beautiful sundial, painting it in the Cherokee manner. He added a painted compass, then protected it with shellac. It's now a unique piece of art that will hopefully withstand another century outside the B&B.

And speaking of the Morning Glory B&B, Ellie Monroe remains the Senior Cat Wrangler, and was given a 100% raise in her salary which she deserves due to her dependability. Based on this, I think she will go far in whatever she chooses as her life's work.

And Hayden and Fiona remain partners in every way, friends and lovers forever - just the way I feel about Janet, even now.

Life in Dublin has moved on without me, as it should. I like to think of this town as one of the trains of old, steaming its way bravely down the tracks, reinventing itself and staying relevant, but in a charming way. Maybe one day in the future (which, as you recall, is non-existent) I'll return physically to the town where I was born and died. But not before Janet and I are done with our travels, and certainly not before Johnny and June Cash go on tour with the Carter Family in the Hereafter!

So there you have it. Dublin will go on, and I hope to see you there one day - but you probably won't see me.

- Dean-

ABOUT THE AUTHOR

Irene Becker has written hundreds of short stories over the years. She lives in a suburb of Memphis, Tennessee, with husband Bill, and Princess, the greyhound. She's also lived in New Jersey, Florida, and Colorado. Always inspired by other writers, she writes in between reading other peoples' books.

Dublin, TN, was first published in 2022. The sequel, *Return to Dublin, TN: Everyday Heroes,* picks up two years later with backstories about original characters, as well as introducing a few new ones in the fictional town of Dublin, Tennessee; after all, it's a city - there are lots of people in a city. Because deceased former mayor Dean Brennan remains interested in the future and well-being of his family, the town, and its inhabitants, he and his wife Janet are frequent visitors. And that's good since their assistance is needed when disaster strikes, threatening the lives of many innocent people.

Postcards From Mom and Other Short Stories, originally published in 2023, is a collection of some of the author's favorite eclectic short stories ranging from humorous to heart-breaking.

All three books are available on many websites. If you purchase them, please leave a comment.

ACKNOWLEDGEMENTS

- Museum of the Cherokee Indian (https://visitcherokeenc.com)

- Eastern Band of Cherokee Indians (https://ebci.com/government

- Many thanks to Kathy Nathan, Eileen Prout, Adam Hobart, and DeVon Frielinger for their excellent comments and suggestions.

- In the book, Dean refers to Enoli as "Didanawisgi", a Cherokee word for medicine man. The following is an extract from <u>Cherokee Medicine</u>:

(https://www.aaanativearts.com/cherokee/cherokee-medicine.htm)

A common thread woven through all Native American remedies is the idea of "wellness" a term recently picked up by some in the modern medical professions. A state of "wellness" is described as "harmony between the mind, body and spirit." The Cherokee word "tohi" - health - is the same as the word for peace. You're in good health when your body is at peace. The "medicine circle" has no beginning and no end and therefore represents a concept of "harmonious unity."

Cherokee medicine is a prevention-based system that incorporates the whole person, rather than the cure-based system that is used by most modern doctors of medicine today, which focuses on the disease. It is the belief among American Indian "doctors" that to achieve wellness we must have a strong connection to all things natural and both create and receive harmony not only within ourselves, but also in all our relationships. Once harmony is restored, illness and other health distortions simply disappear. To some, this would be a "cure." In the Cherokee tradition, this is just good health - the way it should be.

Here the goal is to first help the patient recover - to cure the sickness rather than treat the symptoms - to help the patient find his or her balance - the harmony of our living. The ceremony performed is as important as the potion or salve made from the plants or herbs. This is what is now known as holistic healing - a healing of the complete person.

The United States Pharmacopoeia, which is the modern doctor's drug bible, (companion to the Physician's Desk Reference or PDR - the one that lists all the known side effects of every drug used by modern doctors), first appeared in 1820, and listed over two hundred drugs used by American Indians and acquired from natural plants. Those 200 cures represented 90% of what was listed in that first Pharmacopoeia. Since then, thousands of new drugs have been chemically created in labs which try to replicate and alter the active ingredients in plants already perfected by nature.

Cherokee medicine men and women study for many years, and learn specific treatments from a written Cherokee syllabary given to them by their mentors. It is forbidden for anyone to look at this book if it isn't theirs, and it is often written in code, or parts are passed on verbally to keep the whole from falling into the wrong hands. Medicine ceremonies which are incomplete or performed out of context can do more harm than good, and in the hands of the untrained can be downright dangerous.

Some Cherokee people see only Cherokee medicine people for mental or physical illnesses. Others prefer a combination of treatment from a medicine man and conventional modern medicine. (But) some Cherokees no longer believe in the powers of traditional medicine people.

To the Cherokee, the use of herbs is only one tool of many necessary for regaining one's health. Traditionally it was (and still is) believed that it is crucial to not only heal one's body, mind and spirit, but to reintegrate the ill person with the family, the community and the Earth. This is a holistic perspective beyond our culture's limited understanding. None of us can truly be well unless we recognize our connection to the rest of the Great Life.

ADDENDUM

The following is part of an email from Jakeli Swimmer, MA, Cultural Resource & Archive Officer, Eastern Band of Cherokee Indians, who cautioned the author against including a storyline that partially occurs in the 1870s - a very complicated, ruthless, and sometimes deadly, period of Cherokee history in Eastern Tennessee and surrounds.

"... (In) the timeframe of the 1870s, there was a great deal of change happening and formation within the EBCI and so Cherokee, NC was a completely different place and so was Tribal leadership. Additionally, if Dublin was settled in the 1870s all land was indeed stolen, and it was blatantly stolen from the Cherokee Nation and other tribal nations for centuries... Given the complexities and nuances of our Tribe and its history, regardless of fiction or history, it can be misconstrued and/or romanticized even with the best of intentions."

I sincerely thank Mr. Swimmer for his concern. The real history of our country should never be swept under the carpet no matter what the issue. The history of the United States hasn't always been related in a complete and balanced manner. However you, the reader, realize this is a fictional story about a fictional town with fictional characters, and not a history lesson, right? I intend no disparagement of, or disrespect for, any character or group of people in this book. Thank you for understanding. *-IEB-*

[1] (Note): In the 19th century, the (Cherokee) people had to purchase their land to regain it after it was taken over by the U.S. government through treaty cessions, which had all been negotiated by a small percentage of assimilated Cherokee. *https://en.wikipedia.org/wiki/Eastern_Band_of_Cherokee_Indians*

[2] Ephesians 4:28, New International Version.